THE WESTERN RAIDER:
GUNS OF THE DAMNED

GUNS OF THE DAMNED

By Stone Cody

STEEGER BOOKS • 2020

PUBLISHING HISTORY

"Guns of the Damned" originally appeared in the August/September 1938 (Vol. 1, No. 1) issue of *The Western Raider* magazine. Copyright © 1938 by Popular Publications, Inc. Copyright renewed © 1965 and assigned to Steeger Properties, LLC. All rights reserved.

CHAPTER 1
HELL'S INVADERS

E VEN TODAY along the Border you may hear men
speak of Silver Trent, and whether the rumor of his name
is borne on the breath of good or ill report, always, instinctively,
men speak of him in lowered tones, with a respect which is
close to awe.

In the richly furnished living rooms of great ranches and haci-
endas, the name may be spoken with hatred, but the wild glamor
of the tales which cluster about him will fascinate all who hear
them told. On lonely claims, in the solitary adobe huts of the
poor and underprivileged, or where lean cattle range thin grass
and men fight undaunted for foothold in a harsh land, there
the note of the talk will be different, with throats tightened as
the tales are told, and a deep, long-burning light of gratitude in
remembering eyes.

Or you may hear the legend by lonely campfires along the
dim trails, where hard men curse, in admiration or in fear, at
this name freighted with the sparkle of pure courage, of lawless
daring, of skill and brilliance beyond the reach of ordinary men.

But you would not be likely to hear it spoken today in the
tone of loathing and contempt with which Jim Clane muttered
it that night as he pushed, white-faced, into the squalid, ill-lit
cantina where Lars Johanssen towered above the bar and the
Mexicans who grouped around it. For Jim Clane held Silver

Trent responsible for a good many things, none of them pleasant, and especially for what had happened to Dave Dennison.

Silver slapped a shot in answer as, with a
sudden yell, the charge burst into sight—
more than half a hundred men, rifles and
sixguns spitting a storm of bullets.

He thrust his way through the crowd, hardly seeing the surly
glances that ripped at him, and took his place beside Lars.

"I found Dave," he said out of the corner of his mouth. "They
got him in jail here, and they're goin' to shoot him at sun-up."

Lars Johansen's great hand seemed to bite, white-knuckled,
into the wood of the bar. He cursed, and half-turned toward
the door, his broad, high-cheeked face blazing with anger. Jim
Clane's hand stopped him quickly. "Take it easy," he said through

tight lips, "there's nothin' we can do now. Don't give the game away."

The big Swede stood for a long moment, still undecided, shaken by the sudden berserk fury which had come up in him. "If I get my hands on that Silver Trent," he said thickly, "I break his neck yust like a rabbit."

Next to the pair, a vulture-faced Mexican shot them a quick glance out of his one good eye, then transferred his glance to his drink again, his face gone wooden.

"Listen," Jim Clane said, low-voiced, "this is goin' to take some thinkin'. The jail is set in the middle of a big yard, with a high wall around it. The's only one gate, as far as I can make out, an' that's got two guards on it—one inside an' one out. An' a bunch of greaser soldiers is quartered inside the yard. The's another guard walkin' aroun' the jail itself. It looks like there isn't any way to take care of the three guards without bringin' the *soldados* swarmin' onto us."

"To hell wit' dem," Johanssen snapped. "A bonch of greasers. We take dat yail apart. You don' tank we let Dave die?"

Jim's mouth tightened. "You know damn well that ain't what I mean," he said. "We got to have a plan, is all."

He stood, grim-faced, frowning at the bar in front of him—a blocky, red-headed youngster, with a reckless tilt to his head and twin guns tied low on his thighs. He was fighting to control the heat of the temper in him. This was no time, he knew, to go off half-cocked. That jail was close to being unbreakable, and Dave Dennison was to be stood against the side of the jail, inside that high wall, and shot by a squad of soldiers. At dawn! It was already getting on to midnight.

Dave Dennison and Lars Johanssen and Jim Clane had been partners and saddlemates almost as long as they could remember. They had been riding for Mort Jenkins of the Lazy J, when a series of raids had broken out all through the Big Bend country. At first the raids had appeared unorganized, then it became apparent that there was some sort of plan behind them. Some one man or gang was directing all of them.

Dave Dennison, who spoke Spanish without accent, had volunteered to go into Mexico to try to get information that would enable the Texans to have the gang broken up by the Mexican Rurales. Jim and Lars had wanted to go with him, but Mort Jenkins had forbidden it. A week after Dave had gone in, they had word from him that he believed the raids were directed by an outlaw named Silver Trent; then there was silence.

Jim and Lars waited, chafing with impatience, as the days dragged on. Then, unable to bear it any longer, they had gone into Mexico without permission, leaving no word for Mort Jenkins. The herd they were guarding was in charge of four men altogether, and their departure left the other two on duty alone. They thought that was sufficient. Their hope was to get back before Jenkins even discovered their absence.

THEY FIGURED that Dave had been killed or taken prisoner by this Silver Trent—and they meant to find their friend, or kill his murderer!

The trail had led them here—to this town of Sangre, in the foothills of the Sierras. Along the way, they had asked everywhere for Silver Trent, and had been met by sudden, wooden silence. Bartenders, peons, goat-herders in the hills, had shrugged with veiled eyes and said: *"No lo conosco, señores."*

That repeated phrase, "I don't know him," had filled them with growing, helpless anger, but it had also convinced them that Dave Dennison had been right in his suspicions. This Trent seemed to have the whole countryside in his pocket. He was undoubtedly back of the murder and pillage that had struck in Texas.

Believing that, they felt certain that Trent was behind Dave's imprisonment and impending execution. Trent could evidently do what he liked in this section of Mexico. No doubt he had bought the local officials, to legalize his murders, where it seemed advisable. He had been too yellow to face Dave's guns, so....

With these thoughts smoldering in him, Jim began slowly to talk, trying to outline a plan, trying to cool Lars' mind down to the point where he could be of help. So absorbed were they, that neither noticed the one-eyed Mexican at their side, who seemed broodingly absorbed in his endless drink. They didn't see the faint, cruel smile which shadowed his lips from time to time, did not notice when he paid for his drink and left.

They were not even aware that the room had gone suspiciously quiet and that they were suddenly almost alone at the bar. They had gotten accustomed to the fact that almost no one in this hill country spoke English, and anger had dulled in Jim Clane a trouble-sense which was normally alert and beautifully sensitized.

The Mexican who sidled up to them then had to speak twice before they heard him.

"Is ver' bad here, Señores," he murmured in broken English. "You mus' go *muy pronto*—ver' queek."

Jim Clane swiveled toward him, his gaze sharpening.

"Where do you horn in, hombre?" he asked abruptly.

The Mexican shrugged, made an apologetic gesture with his hands. "I know, Señor," he said. "You mus' go queek—bad trobble *aqui.*"

Jim Clane's eyes narrowed. He could not make this one out. The Mexican was evidently of the peon class—part Indian, maybe. Taller than average, his gaunt shoulders were hunched under a voluminous serape, and one of them hung lower than the other—twisted, as though at one time he had been badly injured. He did not look directly at Jim, so that only his brown cheek and grayed hair under a big straw sombrero were visible. And almost at once he moved away, on bare, dirty feet, walking with a limp.

The one-eyed man had come back and was standing in the doorway.

THE ROOM had gone suddenly silent. Jim Clane's trouble sense was awake now, buzzing. His glance ripped around the cantina, picking out with swift comprehension the figures of half a dozen men who stood out from the others, a sense of tension in their attitudes, their glances veiled yet smoldering. Men in the garb of *vaqueros,* gun-freighted, bristling with knives.

As he looked, three more drifted in—townsmen these, in boleros and concha-hung trousers that flared at the hip. But they also were armed, and every bit as deadly looking as the others.

Jim's spine crisped and went cold. Gun-trap! Was it for them? If it was, there wasn't much chance of getting out with their skins. He cursed himself for a blind fool for having let this creep up on him.

Gracia

He glanced up at Lars Johanssen. The big Swede had evidently become aware of the situation. Like Jim, he had turned his back to the bar, was facing the room with a half-smile of contempt on his big mouth. Jim thought of urging a run for the door, but the door was blocked now. They had waited too long.

Anyway, he doubted if Lars would have gone. The big man's temper was up, and he was in no mood for running from Mexicans. There wasn't anything stupid about Lars, really—but he had one blind spot. He didn't seriously believe that anything or anybody could hurt him. Much less a crowd of greasers!

But Jim Clane, who was just as brave but did not suffer from the stupidity of fearlessness, knew better.

The one-eyed Mexican had drifted over to stand against the wall near the crippled peon who had spoken to Jim. Now, at a glance from him, a pock-marked, rowdy, heavy-set Mex, who had taken on sudden signs of drunkenness, detached himself from a group in a corner and came staggering toward the bar.

Jim Clane laughed suddenly, aloud—but there was no mirth in the laughter. The thing was going to be so obvious and clumsy.

8

The old, old trick of the drunk who jostles somebody and starts the fight which will loose treacherous guns and sudden death. Why in hell didn't they just drag iron and start shooting?

Clane set himself quietly, his hands hanging near the glistening butts of the twin Colts.

Suddenly, the crippled peon spoke to the one-eyed man. "Señor, you will be making a mistake. Many Americans have followed these two—I, Juan, have seen them. If you kill these, they will ride into this town and much blood will flow."

He had spoken in a low, whining tone, but clearly enough for Jim, who spoke Spanish fluently, to hear and understand him.

The one-eyed man turned on the peon with a snarl. "You lie; dog of a *paisano*," he grated. "The roads are watched, and there are no other Americans. What were you saying to those men at the bar? And what do you mean by lying?"

"Señor," the cripple whined, "I am but a poor man, and I tell only what I saw…."

"I think you see too much," the one-eyed man spat wickedly. "From now on, hog, you will see—less!"

His hand flashed to the heavy pearl-handled Colt at his hip. It was a movement as unexpected and venomous as the dart of a rattler's head, and the blaze in his eyes was pure, sudden murder.

Jim Clane caught his breath, his hands flicking gunward in an instinctive movement. Then the caught breath went out of him in a quick rush. For the crippled peon's hands had moved, in a small, half-invisible movement like a man crossing his palms on his breast, and there were guns in them, as though they had grown there by magic.

Colt thunder crashed deafeningly on the silence of the room. The one-eyed man's body jerked. His jaw fell slack. The hand holding his gun drooped, dropped to his side. Then he crumpled, as though he had broken in half.

A babble of curses snarled in Spanish lifted under the gun-echo. Hands raced toward holstered guns and knives.

The cripple had not waited for the one-eyed man to fall. He had whirled, his movements unbelievably fast, and now the rocking thunder of his guns filled the room. A *vaquero* with his Colt cleared of leather coughed wetly and buckled at the knees. Another spun and sat in a nearby chair, clownishly, his hand still clawed at the holster of his shoulder-gun and his face a sudden smear of red.

Jim Clane saw that in the fringe of his vision, without really seeing it. His own Colts were bucking now against his palms, dealing lead for the bolero-ed trio near the door.

CHAPTER 2
GARDEN OF BLACKNESS

THE CANTINA was howling pandemonium. Gun-thunder crashed in a constant, insane hell of sound. Powdersmoke curled upward, acrid, choking, turning the light of the two lamps a dim orange. The screams and curses of angry and frightened men made a crazy counterpoint for the crashing symphony of the guns. Lars Johanssen's fighting bellow cut even above the concussion of the Colts.

Behind Jim Clane, the bartender lifted a wary head, then

his hand flashed upward. The blade of a knife glittered. Lars Johanssen cursed. His great hand shot out, caught the knife as it drove downward.

Two quick shots, one like an echo of the other, smashed the lamps, and blackness dropped on the room in a shower of broken glass. In the startled moment of silence that followed, the crack of the bartender's broken wrist sounded loud, and his scream of pain like a banshee wail.

A hand was on Jim Clane's arm, a voice snapped in his ear. "Get goin', hombre. Through the door, fast, and run to your right."

Colt-fire stabbed the gloom, the muzzle flame driving toward the place where the crippled Mexican had been crouching. But there was no movement there.

Jim caught Lars by the arm. "Out!" he whispered, and jumped for the door.

They hurtled out into the star-spangled darkness of the street. Behind them came the figure of the crippled Mexican.

Jim cursed suddenly under his breath, in wonder. He knew abruptly this was the man who had told him to get out of the cantina, and told it in good clear American! And still he couldn't believe it. For the man who ran at their side, barefooted, in ragged cotton pants, was no longer stooped, no longer carried one shoulder lower than the other, no longer limped. He was tall now, nearly as tall as Lars, big shouldered, and he ran with the swift, feral grace of a timber-wolf.

A babble of excited Mexican voices shrilled behind them.

11

"What is happening?" "Death to the Americans." "Kill the gringo dogs."

Jim Clane cursed again under his breath. The town was up about their ears like a hornet's nest. He would never have believed that a mere barroom brawl would cause so much fuss. But the moment he thought that, he knew that this had not been a mere barroom brawl. There had been a lot more than that behind it. But what, he did not know.

The big man in the serape and ragged pants breathed, "This way," and darted into an alley. He turned twice more, running silently and so swiftly that Jim found his breath coming in painful gasps as he tried to keep up.

Abruptly, the Mex-American stopped. "Up over the wall," he whispered. "Pronto! We mustn't be seen going in here."

Before Jim a blankness of high adobe reared. His jaw dropped a little. Over that wall? They'd need wings. But the man who led them had stooped, was holding locked hands low for Jim's foot.

"Up and make no noise."

Jim stepped in the hand-stirrup held out to him, and felt himself lifted, shooting upward, impelled by a thrust of muscles that seemed unbelievable in its swift, easy power. He caught the edge of the wall, pulled himself up. A fraction of a second later, Lars was beside him.

"Reach your hands down for me," the man below hissed.

He stood off from the wall, took three swift paces forward and jumped. One of his bare feet caught on the wall's surface, seemed to cling, then his powerful hands caught at Lars. The

12

next instant the man's lean body was beside them and the three dropped inside the wall, into the dark stillness of a garden.

A HOUSE with a cupola showed a faint adobe glimmer through the night, and light from an opened doorway struck a shaft across a bed of cannas. From the darkness at the rear of the house a voice called softly, yet with a note of sharpness in it, "*Quien es?*"

The man who had led them said, "Juan?"

A sharply indrawn breath made itself heard in the silence. "Señor!" Juan's voice had a respect in it close to servility. Yet there was something almost like joy in it, too. He came forward at once.

"We need horses, Juan," the big man in the serape told him swiftly. "Go find Don Paolo at the arroyo by the swinging bridge. Tell him to bring my mount and two others to the alley by the Casa Amarilla. And let him take care not to be seen. Go quickly now."

The Mexican bowed. "*Sí, señor—instantamente.*" He was gone like a shadow.

The big man turned to Jim and Lars. "We'll get clear of here," he said reassuringly. "You two hole up here in the garden. I'm goin' into the house a minute."

"Hey, wait a while," Jim said quickly. "We're obliged to you, but we ain't leaving town."

The man in the serape halted, surprise in the quick turn of his head. Then he laughed softly. "You don't quite understand, my friend," he murmured. "Your lives aren't worth a plugged nickel in this town."

"Mebbe so," Jim began suddenly, "but…."

He was interrupted by the appearance of a short, befrocked figure in the lighted doorway.

"Amigo mio!" the newcomer exclaimed softly, at sight of the man in the serape.

He came forward instantly, the doorway light revealing him as a priest, sturdy of build, with legs which looked a little bowed under his cassock, and with a solid paunch that spoke of good living. Nearer, Jim's dark-accustomed eyes made out his round, jovial looking face topped by a shaven pate about which a fringe of fine white hair glimmered like a halo.

"Padre Pete!" Their rescuer's voice had deepened with affection.

Jim Clane's mouth tightened grimly, and with a little irritation. Who the deuce was this big hombre who dressed like a peon, who spoke English like an American, whom servants fawned to and leaped to obey, who handled a gun like the devil himself, yet whose very sight brought this light of pleasure to the face of a priest?

"We're in a jackpot, Padre," the man said swiftly. "Sorry to come here, but there wasn't much of anywhere to come. We'll get out without gettin' you into any trouble."

"That is with God, *amigo,*" the priest said tranquilly. "You know that you are always welcome here."

Lars Johanssen nudged Jim. "We got durn little time," he muttered. "We got to do somethin'."

Jim Clane said quickly, politely, "If you'd let us hide out just

14

Johanssen's great hand blurred to his gun, came up freighted with death.

a little while in your garden, Padre—until things quiet down. We got to—"

The man in the serape cut him off. "Not a minute longer than necessary," he said curtly. "If we're found here, it will be serious for Padre Pedro. We go the instant the horses are there."

THE QUIET authority in his tone grated on Jim Clane's nerves.

"You don't get it, hombre," he rapped out. "We got a friend in jail in this town. They're shootin' him at dawn. We ain't leaving without takin' him with us."

The big man shrugged. "I've heard about your friend," he said quietly. "But believe me, it's impossible for you to do anything now. You've run against El Diablo, and—"

He broke off as a girl appeared in the doorway—a girl who had a swaying grace of carriage such as Jim Clane had never seen—and who cried, "Silver!" in a low voice that vibrated with joy.

Silver? Jim Clane swung on the man, his mouth hard, his eyes narrowed by suspicion.

"Silver? You wouldn't be Silver Trent, now would you?" His voice burred.

The big man smiled in the darkness. "That's what I'm called," he acknowledged.

Something like a snarl ripped out of Lars Johanssen's throat. His great hand blurred to his gun, came up freighted with death.

The man in the serape had taken one swift step forward. Now his left hand caught Lars' gun while his right moved like a short flash of lightning. It made an invisible arc and chopped down so that the edge of the palm landed on the muscle of Lars' forearm.

The big Swede grunted with the paralyzing pain of it and his fingers loosened on the gun. It came loose into Silver Trent's left hand. And then it lifted, settled with a dull plop against Lars' head behind his right ear.

Jim Clane cursed, and drove for his guns. The thing had been so fast, and that liquid flow of movement so uninterrupted, that it had caught him off guard.

But when he did move, it was with a speed which had already made his guns famous above the border.

They came ripping up as Silver Trent whirled and came toward him.

Jim Clane's mouth was a white, bitter line and his mind a cold deadliness. When he started this draw, he had meant to take Silver Trent prisoner. But the man had the supple speed of a panther. He was already moving in on Jim before the latter's guns had cleared leather—moving in with that gun in his hand yet not leveled, as though he had no intention of shooting. But Jim Clane had no intention of being taken either.

The instant he had heard that name—Silver Trent—his mind had blazed with the understanding of the man's treachery. No wonder Trent was so bent on getting them out of town. He didn't want Dave Dennison rescued! Now, if Jim Clane let the same thing happen to himself as had happened to Lars....

His fingers tightened on the triggers as his muzzles flashed upward. Even in that second his racing mind knew that it was touch and go as to whether Trent, sidestepping in, would be able to knock his right gun aside before he could fire it at him.

His muscles jerked with the effort of speed. His mind was a fierce tension, locked in the grip of one thought: "Kill! Kill Silver Trent!"

Something flashed into view at the fringe of his vision. Knuckles, whitened, growing with the speed of a comet. Behind them, a cassock-covered shoulder, driving!

Instinctively he flinched, tried to duck. Something exploded under his ear. White light blazed in his brain. The light seemed to burst outward, through holes in his skull. Then it flashed back, as though drawn by a powerful suction pump, and blackness flooded in after it. He knew no more....

CHAPTER 3
PRISONER

THE JOLT of a trotting horse punched Jim Clane back into consciousness. For a moment, his mind was confused and his head joggled from side to side. Then memory came back to him and he straightened, cursing.

The man holding his arm released it with a sigh. "May God forgive me, amigo," he said piously in Spanish, "but you were growing heavy!"

Jim glanced at him in surprise. He had expected from the beginning of that sentence to find the priest beside him, but this was another man entirely.

Could it be Don Paolo? He remembered Silver Trent's

instructions to the servant, Juan. The dim light showed him a thin, melancholic face, decorated by a thin beard and mustache and with a forehead which showed high and somehow fanatic looking even under the brim of the wide, concha-jingling sombrero.

Ahead were two other horsemen, both big men, with one of them supporting the other. Silver Trent and Lars.

Jim jerked a hand to reach for a gun, and cursed. His wrists were bound.

"Where in hell are you takin' us, you damn side-windin' snakes?" he snarled.

"Quiet, Señor." The melancholy Mexican's voice sounded hurt. "They're still on our trail. Listen."

From far behind, Jim heard faint shouts and the single shot of a gun, as though somebody had fired at a shadow.

"What's it to me?" Jim rapped out. "I'd as soon be taken by one gang of murderers as another."

"Señor," the Mexican told him softly. "If you are not quiet, I will have to hit you on the head again, which God forbid. For violence, like sin, is hateful to me."

There was something in the man's gentle, melancholy tone which told Jim that he meant exactly what he said. He began to feel slightly mad. This night was beginning to be too fantastic for him. First, a peon who turned out to be a gunfighting fool, then was revealed as being one whom men worshiped, to judge by their manner and voices, and was finally transformed into a raiding, murdering outlaw whose very name was a curse in Jim's mind. Add to him a jolly priest with a right cross like the kick of

19

a mule and a girl who watched fast and deadly action without a gasp. That was plenty in itself. But on top of it a bandit who announced himself as hating violence as he hated sin…!

It made Jim Clane dizzy. And he was that already. His head rang and ached as though the hammers of hell were going in it, and his jaw and neck under his ear felt sore and swollen. He didn't believe, suddenly, that he had been hit by a fist.

"What did that accursed priest sock me with?" he muttered in Spanish.

The Mexican drew in his breath with a hiss. "Accursed priest!" His hand flicked, and was suddenly jabbing a knife, with a long and wicked blade, directly at Jim's chest.

Jim tried to throw himself from the saddle, and discovered then, for the first time, that his feet were tied under the horse's belly.

The Mexican checked the knife a few inches from Jim's heart, and seemed to hesitate. "No," he murmured, "the good father himself would not like it." He returned the blade to its sheath. "But do not try me too far, Señor," he said. "What you said is blasphemy, and my patience is not long."

They rode in silence for perhaps ten minutes, during which Jim became aware that there were horses immediately behind him. Then, surprisingly, the melancholy man chuckled, and spoke in broken English. "You don' like the box-fight, Señor? Padre Pedro he mak' ver' good the box-fight."

Ahead, Silver Trent pulled up. "What do you think, Paolo," his voice came murmuring through the night, "have we thrown them off?"

The melancholy man shrugged. "Those fools who yelled, perhaps," he answered. "But that Sancho is like a dog of the hunt. Even at night, he will smell the very trace of a trail."

He slid from the saddle and lay with an ear pressed to the ground for a long time.

Jim Clane glanced at the two horses that had pulled up behind him. One of them was ridden by a Mexican he had never seen before. The other carried a limp body tied across the saddle.

Paolo got up, nodding gravely. "They are coming," he said. "May the saints have mercy on our souls and theirs!"

Silver Trent turned his horse. "No more talking!" His voice was the mere ghost of a sound, like an eddy within the soft night breeze, gone before it had even sounded, yet the effect of it was like a command clanging out on steel.

JIM CLANE set his lips grimly. The authority in this man's voice roused all his antagonism. Yet, he was aware with sudden shame, he had no stomach whatever for trying to talk.

Lars Johanssen, he saw, had come to his senses and was riding without assistance. But even Lars did not attempt to say anything. Jim knew that the big Swede must be boiling with anger, so that made this a record. There never had been a time before when anybody had kept Lars quiet when he was mad.

Full sanity began to come back to Jim. It was plain enough that Silver Trent did not intend to kill him and Lars. At least, not at once. What did he want of them, then? To hold them for ransom?

A wry, mirthless grin came to Jim's lips at that thought. He could imagine Mort Jenkins paying out any good money for their hides! Trent had a disappointment coming to him if that was what he counted on. But meanwhile there might be a chance to get away, turn the tables.

It occurred to Jim suddenly, then, that all this depended on whether or not they got away from whoever was following them. And who the devil would that be? A Mex town might conceivably get on its ear because of a little shooting, but he had never heard of one that would track the perpetrators of a brawl so persistently through the night. Stuff like that was a lot too much trouble for the average Mex. He remembered then what Silver Trent had said about *El Diablo*, but the name was meaningless to him.

As his head cleared, the tension began to grow in him again intolerably. He did not know what time it was, but it was long after midnight, and from the feel of the air sunup could not be more than an hour or two away. And at sunup Dave Dennison would die.

Jim began to pray that whoever was behind them would catch up. If there was a fight, he might be freed, to use his guns. Or if not, in the confusion, he could get away. Now, tied to his horse, with his hands bound behind his back and Paolo holding the reins, he was helpless.

He began to work his wrists. The bonds did not feel very tight. If he could get them loose, he could knock this melancholy, religious-minded greaser on the head and make a break for it. Fifteen minutes later, Silver Trent called another halt, while Paolo again put his ear to the ground. This time the Mexican shook his head.

"No sound," he said briefly.

Either they had lost them completely or the pursuit had fallen behind.

Jim Clane was sweating, his wrists already raw, but he kept straining at the ropes, imagining that he felt them give ever so slightly. After another half an hour of riding, his heart began to hammer with excitement. The bonds were definitely looser. Within ten minutes now, he should be able to....

A sudden turn in the arroyo they were riding, brought them within sight of a campfire, and a song burst at them. Jim heard Silver Trent swear, but he was no longer interested in what Trent felt. His own heart had dropped into his boots. His hands were still not free, and they were in sight of Trent's camp. He could see figures lying or moving about the fire.

A figure rose from the darkness by the trail.

"You, Ben?" Trent snapped. "Why didn't you challenge?"

"I knew the trot of that white horse of your'n, Silver," the guard said, "an' saw the dark star on his chest a hundred yards away. But you was covered all right."

"Keep your ear to the ground, then," Trent said a little grimly. "We're liable to have visitors."

The roaring voice at the campfire had not ceased to sound forth. Sweat rolled down Jim Clane's face as he fought his bonds, and with it he could feel bloody sweat drip from his finger tips. In a minute now, it would be too late.

Then, suddenly, they were within the circle of the campfire, and he slumped in his saddle, exhausted. Behind him, Paolo's voice sounded, making a little sound of pity with his lips.

"What a shame you did not ask, amigo," he said. "I always tie them so that you can take up a little slack, but there was no chance for you to get loose—none at all. May the saints pity your poor wrists!"

Jim cursed him, snarling.

BY THE fire, the man who had been singing was roaring a greeting to Silver Trent.

"Odd's thunder, my brave compadre!" he bellowed. "Well met! You arrive at the crucial, the psychological instant, when Beau and I are about to sample another bottle. It is a relief to me, for I swear to you by my grandfather's britches, that I can no longer tolerate this icicle, this accursed gambler, this bowel-less tinhorn, who insults that noblest beverage, *tequila*, by remaining stone sober on it. 'Pon my honor, 'tis a dishonor that the honor of *tequila* cannot—"

"Sober up, Doc," Silver Trent said quietly. "There's work for you."

The man he spoke to was a florid, powerfully made individual, with a sizable belly, a bristling white mustache and a great nose whose crisscross of veins looked blue-black in the dancing light of the fire. There was a hearty, driving pugnaciousness in the whole set of the big body and it was plain enough that he was lordly drunk.

Jim Clane grinned mirthlessly. It would take more than a word to get this one sober, if he was any judge of boozers.

Some of the nondescript, ragged-looking crew who had been grouped around the fire had gotten up and were loosening the

24

ropes which held the wounded man into the saddle. Jim could hear them cursing bitterly among themselves.

"Sober up?" The man called Doc was gruff, yet somehow placating. "Sober up? Why, man, I have but begun. Sober up? By the britches of grandfather—not before Wednesday a week!"

"Marko's pretty badly hit, Doc." Silver Trent's voice was still quiet, but there was a hint of iron in it. "Sober down if you don't want to sober up—but take care of him."

The doctor boomed a rolling string of high-flown curses and set down the bottle from which he was about to drink. He went staggering over to the wounded man.

"Can't keep out of the way of lead, hey?" he bellowed. "Marko, you were always luckier than brainy, by the...."

He knelt down, nearly falling, and began an examination of the wound. A moment later, he stood up. His entire expression and his voice had changed.

"Get him over to the hut and bring all the lanterns you've got," he said crisply to one of the men who stood at his elbow. "You, Chico, boil water. Careful now," he cautioned, as hands lifted Marko gently, "I'll have the hide of the first man that stumbles or jars him."

He turned briskly away, walking straight and steady. Jim stared after him with dropped jaw. This was as sober a man as he had ever looked at!

Paolo chuckled at his elbow. "You are surprise, eh? Thees hombre she is Doc Brimstone—she is more better *medico* dronk as all de odders sober. *Por Dios, sí!* I tell you mos' true!"

Jim cursed him automatically. His brain felt a little numb.

25

Across the fire he saw the huge form of Lars Johanssen. He had been cut free of his mount and the bonds which held his hands. Lars was standing there motionless, a queer expression on his wide, high-cheekboned face.

Paolo began to untie the ropes around Jim's ankles and wrists. As he worked he talked, abandoning English for his native tongue. In the soft, slurring Mexican Spanish his voice was a murmur full of sadness:

"Ah, but it is a pity to all the saints—he is a profane man—*borrachon* and roisterer. One who speaks without respect of things holy. Even for the goodness he does, I am sometimes afraid the good God will not forgive him. *El Doctor Brimstone!* This is a name of his very nature—yet he has a heart soft as butter! I have burned candles to all the saints—that they preserve him from the fire his name promises."

Jim Clane climbed down from the saddle, and stood swaying a moment on numbed legs. His hands, raw-wristed and streaked with blood were clawed before him, and his eyes were suddenly a little mad.

"You think you can rawhide me—with your damn pious talk and your damn doctors that make out to be orey-eyed when they ain't?" he snarled at the Mexican. "I've had enough of it. By God, one other little word of you, Greaser, an' I'll take you apart so even that fat sawbones can't put you together again."

He was breathing hard and his face was fearfully contorted, as though he were about to burst into tears of rage.

Paolo cast him a look of melancholy astonishment and backed away from him, "*Señor!*" he murmured protestingly.

CHAPTER 4
A CHANCE TO KILL

SILVER TRENT had been talking to a leathery looking oldster with a drooping white longhorn mustache—a man who might have been anywhere from fifty to eighty years old. Out of a wrinkled, ageless face looked a pair of shrewd, bright blue eyes. Vaguely, Jim remembered that someone had called him Magpie. Now, as the man turned away, Trent came over to the fire.

"Clane! Johanssen!" he called curtly. "I want to talk to you."

Jim Clane stood glaring at him, his hands working. This was the devil who was responsible for all their troubles—and responsible for Dave Dennison's death. Yet he commanded them to appear before him as though he was some kind of king—and did not even look to see whether or not they obeyed. He had removed his shirt, and now was sitting down taking off his pants!

A deadly anger boiled up in Jim. He would obey, all right. He'd go and tell this man what he thought of him, and when that was done, he'd kill him with his bare hands.

All coolness and good sense had left him. The things that had happened to him that night and the strain he had been under had been temporarily too much for his mind. He stalked forward with the drawn set face and blazing eyes of a madman.

Silver Trent seemed scarcely to regard him. He had stripped to the skin, and was reaching down into a stack of clothes which someone had brought him for fresh garments. Automatically, Jim noted that Trent's hands and face had been treated with some brown stain, to help his disguise as a Mexican. Where the stain stopped, his skin was marble white, save where the firelight painted it. And under it, such muscles moved as Jim Clane had never seen.

The panther-like power and speed of the man was revealed now at its source, and as he stood up to face Jim and Lars, he made a figure so arresting as to shock even Jim's tortured mind into momentary wonder.

More than six feet, Trent stood. The corded column of his neck ran into wide, sloping shoulders on which the muscles stood out like sculptured marble. The great chest, its depth and capacity almost concealed by the magnificent proportions of the whole torso, ran down into a waist which appeared small only by comparison, and whose ridged armor was like corrugated iron. Powerful loins merged into thighs whose great muscles ran like supple interlocking steel cables into the lower legs. Even the muscles of the feet stood out, ridged and flowing, so that the soles and toes seemed to grip the ground light and easily, but powerfully.

Sudden sobriety flowed into Jim Clane. His idea of killing this man with his hands slid from him like a piece of forgotten nonsense. But the idea of killing him did not. He glanced around quickly, seeking a weapon.

"We're liable to have a fight on our hands," Silver Trent told the two of them curtly. "You can either be tied up an' take your chances, or you can be given your guns to fight with. Which will you choose?"

"Damn you," Jim Clane grated, his eyes blazing pure hatred,

"Give me a gun an' I'll promise to shoot you loose from your backbone. Dave Dennison is dyin' at sunup. If I have my way about it, you'll break trail for him on the way to hell!"

El Diablo

Jim found himself looking all at once into a luminous pair of gray eyes which had, though his anger and hatred tried to deny it, a queerly magnetic power. He realized with a shock that this was the first time he had actually seen Silver Trent. And even in this moment he was able to understand that under other circumstances this lean, clearcut, hawknosed face, with the long, firm mobile lips and wide clear brows, would have made a strong impression on him, and that he would have trusted instinctively the man behind it.

But there was no trust in him now, nothing but a corroding hostility which ate into him all the more bitterly because Trent looked like something he wasn't. To be what he was, and yet have this quiet strength and odd, compelling attractiveness in him only heightened his offense, only made him more completely loathsome. Here was a devil in all-too-human form, who had to be wiped off the face of the earth as mercilessly as a man would stomp on the head of a snake.

JIM CLANE was thinking that with one part of his mind while another part noted that his words appeared to have made no impression on the man before him.

29

Silver Trent's expression was tranquil. There was even a little glint of amusement in the wide-set gray eyes. His lips moved as though he were about to make some answer, but at that moment there was an interruption. The leathery oldster bowlegged up to the fire and said abruptly, "Doc says he's got a chance, an' can't be moved."

Trent's expression changed. "Then we'll be here, Magpie," he said crisply. "Make it as fast as you can."

Jim Clane heard that without hearing, for all at once he had seen it—the gun with which he would kill Silver Trent! It was hying half-concealed in a blanket near the fire. Only a part of the butt and the cylinder was visible, but at the rim of the cylinder the firelight glinted on yellow brass. The gun was loaded, and that was all that Jim Clane wanted to know.

His pulses began to hammer. It would be easy now. He would stall a minute, ask time to think Trent's proposition over. He would squat thoughtfully by the fire, staring into the flames, and then send slug after slug ripping and smashing into that big, deadly, naked body. Jim Clane might die. He might not be able to shoot his way clear. But the world would be rid of Silver Trent!

The leathery hombre—Magpie Myers—was looking worried. "Mebbe ye oughtn't to risk it, Silver. That Marko, he ain't wuth much anyways."

Trent stirred impatiently. "Talk sense, Magpie," he said curtly.

Magpie Myers still hesitated. He looked into the darkness out beyond the fire, his head lifting in a queerly animal gesture, his nose and eyes questing. "I don't like it," he muttered.

He looked like a scarred and lean old wolf standing there, scenting the wind for trouble, and the thought flashed into Jim's mind that he was feeling, with some sixth sense, a death that crept on noiseless feet through the night. Reasonlessly, Jim's spine chilled.

"It's riskin' a lot of good men for one," the oldster went on stubbornly.

"That's part of the game, Magpie," Silver Trent told him quietly. "Get goin'."

Impatiently, Jim shook himself free of the momentary spell the old man had put on him. He took an easy, careless step toward the fire, and the gun.

Silver Trent began to put on his clothes, his face absorbed, as though he had forgotten Lars and Jim.

Jim lounged another couple of steps toward the blaze.

Standing there, he saw that Magpie Myers had joined a group of men, four of five of them, who were mounted. A moment later, they all disappeared silently into the darkness. He wondered where they were going, but left the thought without trying to answer it. So much the better for him. There would be fewer of them to take shots at him when he had killed Trent.

He was about to risk another step in the direction of the gun when Silver Trent's voice swung him, a snarl on his lips.

"You hombres are outlawed now anyway," the outlaw leader tossed at them crisply. "The herd you were with above the border has been stolen, an' the two men you left behind with it have been killed. You're bein' blamed for the robbery and the killing. There's a price on your heads."

31

Lars Johanssen had also begun to sidle toward the fire, as though he thought that Jim was maneuvering for a word with him privately. Now he, too, swung toward Trent, a sound ripping from his throat like the growl of an enraged grizzly.

Jim Clane's fingers bit into his palms. "You lie, you—you—"

Trent's curt voice cut him off. "I'm tellin' you the truth. Take it or leave it. If you go back to your section you'll be jailed, an' maybe lynched. You gave no notice to your boss of where you were goin'. An' your partners can't testify for you, bein' plenty dead. Your best play is to throw in with us."

Fury choked Jim Clane so that he could hardly speak. "You—you sneakin' sidewinder!" he raged. "How do you happen to know about all that? Don't bother to answer—you know it because you took the herd yourself. Like you been takin' all of 'em!"

He stopped, shaking all over. He had to keep himself in hand until he could get to that gun. He had to—had to!

For a moment, Silver Trent's gray eyes were chill, deadly, and the set of his lips flat and tightened. But when he spoke his voice was level.

"I know about it because it's my business to know things," he said evenly. "Same way I've known for the last week that you was travelin' through the country askin' for me. That's part of the reason I was in town tonight—to look you over an' find out what you had on your minds. From what you say, I figger you hold me responsible for Dennison's bein' in jail, an' for the rest of what's been happenin' above the border. But it happens that I'm not.

32

The man you're lookin' for is a *muy* respectable Mex gent that you're liable to run into if you stick by me.

From his tone and words, no one would have supposed that he had just been called a sneaking sidewinder.

JIM TURNED away abruptly toward the fire. The movement brought him within reach of the gun. He squatted, pretending to stare at the flames. His mind was raving. What did this murdering cow-thief take him for—a fool? Did he expect him, Jim Clane, to fall for a thin yarn like that?

His hand flicked out and closed over the butt of the sixgun. The hundredth part of a second later the muzzle pointed across his stomach at Silver Trent.

"You've told your last lie, an' made your last kill, Trent," he rasped. "Get ready to die!"

Silver Trent did not move, did not change expression.

"You can't do it, Jim," he said clearly. "It would be murder."

"Can't I?" Jim snarled, and his finger tightened on the trigger.

Lars Johanssen's big hand flashed out, slamming the muzzle of the gun earthward.

"You damn Judas!" Jim's eyes were murderous. "So you've changed sides, have you?"

Lars' grip on the gun was iron, immovable. "I tank—I tank," he said slowly, " 've haf been wrong."

Jim's laugh was half-hysterical, venomous with contempt. "So you fell for it!" he snapped. "He made you into an outlaw, an' now you've let him make you into a fool."

Silver Trent had still not moved. "Let him go, Lars," he said quietly.

33

The big Swede looked at him with dropped jaw. "What?" There was sheer unbelief in the tone.

"Let him go," Silver repeated quietly. "I put the gun there for him. Let's see if he can use it."

"But—" Lars began, then his great fingers loosened, almost as much from shock, it seemed, as from any will of his own.

"All right, Jim." Silver Trent's voice was suddenly vibrant. "Now's your chance. Do you think you can take it?"

Jim Clane snapped to his feet. He was trembling all over. "So it was a trick!" He snarled bitterly. "Either you lie, or the gun has dummy loads."

"No lie!" Trent ripped back at him. "The gun will kill if you can pull the trigger. Can you?"

"By God, you'll see!" The sixgun snapped up, leveled square at Silver Trent's heart. Jim's eyes narrowed over the sights.

Silver Trent stood silent, waiting. There was no flicker of fear in his eyes, no tension now about the even, pleasant line of his mouth. He looked like a spectator watching an interesting experiment. Or like a gambler, in love with the game, watching the turn of a card. Only this time the card would decide either for life—or death.

Time by the fireside seemed to stand still. Jim Clane's jaws locked. Sweat stood out on his brow. In the shadows, the fringe of his vision showed that the scene had attracted the attention of others of the gang. He thought, "I've got to shoot fast, or someone will get me first."

His trigger finger tensed, locked in some queer paralysis.

The veins on his forehead stood out like a man straining to lift a great weight.

The gun shook, wavered. With a broken curse, he flung it to the ground.

"You win, damn you!" he choked. "I can't do it. Not that way."

He stood with bowed head, every nerve and muscle in him shaking with reaction.

Silver Trent went to him swiftly. His hand fell on Jim's shoulder. "Take it easy, *amigo*," he said, and his voice was vibrant and warm. "You've been too worked up. Seein' it from your point of view, it must have looked tough. Forget it. I didn't want to tell you before, but I've sent some of the boys out to get Dave Dennison. I don't promise they'll do it. But if it can be done at all, they're the jaspers to pull it off."

Jim stared up at him, still fighting unbelief, still not able to adjust himself to having nothing to hate. "You—you mean that? You swear to that?"

"That's where Magpie an'—"

The echoing blast of a sixgun ripped the silence of the night into howling shreds.

CHAPTER 5
ON THE RIM

S ILVER TRENT cursed. "He let them creep on him. I was a fool…." Trent whirled. "Arturo! The fire!"

His hand swooped, swung his gunbelt around his hips. A jump carried him to the gun Jim had dropped. He grabbed it up, "Your guns are the other side of the fire," he snapped. "Get them on the jump!"

A Mexican came running with two pails of water. The fire keened, sputtered, broke into steam, and then was a blackening glow of drenched ashes. A gun lanced flame from the rim of the depression in which the camp lay. Lead snapped, howling, past Jim Clane's ear.

Silver Trent's guns bucked and bellowed in his hands. From the rim where the flame-flower had bloomed and died a pulpy, coughing cry sounded.

Guns hammered now from all around the rim of the depression—a hell of rattling fire that swept the campsite with lead. Jim Clane had his guns now. The feel of them in his hands, the familiar, sweet balance of them, sent a savage joy into him. He didn't know how bad this scrap was going to be and he didn't care.

It was action, straight and direct, and the sudden relief from his perplexities made him feel a little drunk.

"Come an' get it, ma honeys!" he yelled, and sent lead smashing at the winking gun-flashes along the rim.

The guns of all Trent's gang were hammering answer to the

GUNS OF THE DAMNED

Silver Trent

attackers now. The basin had exploded into a pandemonium of Colt thunder, the yells and curses of fighting men, and, from time to time, low but audible under the storm, the *thunk!* of lead into flesh and the groaning outgo of breath as a man crumpled.

On his belly, Jim Clane emptied his guns, rolling after every few shots, first to one side, then to the other. Bullets bit at him through the darkness. The vicious whine of questing lead was like a constant song in his ears. With hurried fingers he crammed fresh cartridges into the hot cylinders of his guns.

On his right, the deep-throated fighting laughter of Lars Johanssen sounded. He wondered how long the laughing would last. Lars could stand only so much give-and-take of bullet exchange. Mostly he went berserk before the end, threw his guns at the enemy and waded in with his hands. Gunfighting was all right, but for Lars nothing took the place of feeling his enemy under those big, rawboned hands of his.

To the left of him, a steady stream of blasphemy in Spanish was sounding. Jim grinned, thinking that such language was enough to make a man's hair curl. And then, as a roll brought him in that direction, his jaw dropped open and one of his shots must have gone completely wild. For the man who was cursing with such vivid eloquence was Paolo, the Pious! And as he cursed, his guns beat a hell's tattoo of death!

Jim pressed his lips into a straight line, but this time a grin kept tugging at them. What kind of outfit was this he had gotten into, where men alternated between apparently sincere religiousness and impious language that would blister the skin of the devil; where doctors were roaring drunk and then sober as judges within the space of fifteen seconds? Where the leader sent much-needed men off to help a stranger, and where a whole gang stayed and put their lives in jeopardy because one man was too badly hurt to move! What kind of outlaws, in God's name, were these?

Jim's heart warmed and swelled suddenly, half in shame because of what he had thought of them, half in pride because he was fighting shoulder to shoulder with them.

And they were fighters! No mistake about that. The firing had already begun to die down because the gang on the rim was dropping back, taking cover, instead of coming forward. Yet, estimating from the gun-flashes, there must be nearly a hundred of them—against maybe twenty!

FOR A time—Jim could not guess how long—the situation remained about static. Shots still came from the rim and were answered from the darkness below, But there was no more of the first wild firing.

The chill of before-dawn was in the air. It wouldn't be so many minutes now before the first gray came into the east.

Somebody walked on swift, cat-quiet feet up to him and stopped, saying "Take cover, but keep clear of the corral. They're waiting for sunup, so they'll have us under their guns. We'll give 'em a little surprise."

It was Silver Trent, his voice so low that it was no more than a stir in the dark quiet, but clear enough to be heard. Jim would have sworn that it would not have been audible six inches beyond his own ear.

Quietly, he began to move back, searching for cover. There

was a wonder in him over this Trent. He had never before known a man like him. Had he really left that gun there for him to use? It didn't make sense. Why? And yet somehow the conviction rode him that that was exactly what Silver Trent had done.

A clump of brush loomed up on his right, and he took cover behind it. He understood suddenly that when daylight came, anybody in the basin who was at all exposed would be at a bad disadvantage. He'd make a full-length target, even lying down, for the crowd on the rim to shoot at, whereas only their heads would show. And who were *they*, in God's name?

Lars slid in at the other side of the bush, moving with remarkable quiet for a man of his bulk. That was another mystery. What had happened to Lars, to tame him as he was? He not only had believed in Silver Trent, but he acted as if he was already under the man's domination.

Jim edged over until he could talk into Lars' ear. "I wish to God I knew what this was all about," he whispered.

"Silver said somethin' about a greaser back of it," Lars murmured. "Whoever it is, I'll bet he needs hangin'."

"Silver says!" Jim breathed. "How come you're so shore everythin' Silver says is the mustard?"

Lars shook his head. "I naver see a man before that can take me like that," he muttered, as though that was somehow an explanation. Then his teeth glimmered whitely through the dark in a wide grin. "My ol' man, he say the only way I ever learn somethin' is be hit over head with hammer. Maybe that vork also with gun-barrel."

Jim chuckled aloud, and brought lead from the rim ripping

through the bushes. He shot three times at the flash, but apparently missed.

It started the shooting going again, and for a moment the air around him sounded like it was swarming with night-flying hornets. Night-flying? The stars were now beginning imperceptibly to pale.

His chest began to feel tight, with a quick beat of pulse in it. In a little, it would be dawn. What was happening to Dave Dennison? Had Silver told the truth? And would Magpie succeed? For a moment, he forgot the deadly danger he himself, with the rest of them, would be in as soon as the darkness thinned.

Again there was that cat-like tread of Silver Trent's and his voice murmuring: "Slide over to the corral now. There's a horse saddled for you."

Then he was gone, like the shadow of some roving jungle beast. Jim felt a twinge of disappointment. Were they going to give up? Had Silver decided to abandon Marko?

With Lars at his side, he got to his feet and moved softly off to obey. The whole gang was there—ready to ride. Jim cursed softly. Somehow he felt like it was a personal affront. He hadn't thought this Silver would let himself be run off with his tail between his legs.

Next to him, Paolo swung into the saddle. "We ride to rim," he whispered. "Begin at thees end—r-roll dem up like tamale. You follow me, *por Dios*. We mak' plenty fon!"

JIM'S SHOULDERS went up. This was going to be all right! The rim made a semi-circle around the camp, the other side of the basin being formed by a high bluff, apparently. He didn't have the lay of the land very well in his mind, having ridden in at night, but at least he knew that the firing had been confined to a half circle. The ground sloped up sharply to this rim from the basin, but not so sharply that a horse couldn't be ridden up it.

Evidently, Silver meant to ride up, take that half-circle on one end, then ride all the way around it, a kind of charge by the flank. It was a daring move, and if it worked, it would put considerable confusion into the enemy ranks.

"Now! Ride!" Silver's voice rapped out.

Jim saw his horse jump forward under the sharp bite of the spurs, had a glimpse of the wide shoulders straight in the saddle, and then in a sudden roar of hoofs, the whole group was in head-long motion. For a priceless second there was silence from the rim. It was evident that the attackers were taken off guard by this move, did not realize what was happening. Then, straight ahead, the guns opened up.

Silver Trent's guns blasted answer, then other guns in the front of the charge. Suddenly the rim of the basin seemed to blaze into a sheet of flame, as the other attackers jerked out of their daze into action.

Ahead of Jim, a horse went down. His own horse swerved wildly, and for a breathless instant Jim thought he would not get clear. But he did clear, and swift pressure on the rein brought him back into the line of the charge.

Jim felt the ground lift sharply under his mount's feet, then they were driving up the slope, the muscles of the bronc lifting and thrusting under him like laboring pistons.

To the right, a saddle emptied, but the horse went on. A sixgun blared in Jim's face, the bullet burning his cheek. He slammed a slug into a crouching figure and saw the man straighten, plunging outward from the rim.

Trent was on the rim now and had wheeled his horse with a yell, charging straight along the rim. Jim cut sharply to the left on the slope and drove steel to his mount. He was not going to be left forever in the rear of this action.

The movement was a short-cut which brought him to the rim just three men after Silver Trent. One of those men, he saw with a grin, was Paolo, who had worked the same trick as himself.

The other side of the rim, he saw now for the first time, was also a slope, but gentler. There was room to spread out. He cut in, riding diagonally down-slope and then forward, to get abreast of the others. He made it, for Silver Trent was not riding at a dead run now. He had pulled down to a gallop to give his blazing guns time to clear the way before him.

Behind Jim, Lars' berserk roar lifted, "Stand an' take it, snakes!" And beside him Paolo rolled his bellowing, gargantuan blasphemies to the shocked and paling skies.

A figure lifted out of the dimness before Jim, hesitated, tried to run, then turned desperately to fire. Jim's right gun lifted, came arcing down to land with a sickening smash on the man's skull. Ahead, another stood erect, a Winchester leveled at Jim's chest. Too late, Jim swung his gun to fire, but Paolo's sixgun racketed. The Winchester swung skyward, exploding, and the man who had held it disappeared underfoot.

Running figures filled the thinning dusk now as the men who

had held the rim broke in panic and scurried down the slope. They were nearly helpless before this charge, unable to shoot until the Trent men were on top of them, for fear of hitting their own men.

Even so, they might have swung out and made shift to blast down that bunched and racing target, if they had kept their heads. But the thing had been too fast for them, those thundering hoofs and savage yells too terrifying. They broke in complete disorder and ran, down the slope.

Lars Johanssen, his big voice a mad chant of war, had ridden up alongside Jim, on the right. Now his racing horse cut off one of the men who was trying to run. With a yell, the man turned sideways, snapping a Colt-shot at the huge figure leaning over him. Lars' great hand reached out, caught him, lifted him, sent his pinwheeling body sailing in a great arc to land with a smashing thud on the camp side of the rim!

CHAPTER 6
KIDNAPPED

IT WAS seeing that whirling body go kiting past against the sky that made Jim realize that dawn was really there. And then, all at once, they were at the far end of the rim.

Trent had pulled up, one hand lifted to signal a halt.

"Nice ridin', boys," he laughed. "Now, down the slope here, dismount, and line the rim. Pronto!"

He sent his horse plunging back down the sharp slope toward the camp.

Then Jim got it, and cursed in admiration. For a moment, he had wondered why Silver had not led his men on the heels of the routed enemy, but a second thought told him that this would have been to invite destruction. They were still outnumbered by three or four to one. They would have had to scatter, and scattering, they would have been wiped out by men who would have been fighting with the desperation of cornered rats, from cover, with big targets to shoot at, and a growing light to shoot by.

This way the situation would be exactly reversed. It would be the Trent men who would be shooting from the cover of the rim now, down-slope at an enemy who would have to cross the open to get at them. The purpose of that charge had been to clear the rim and to give the Trent men an overwhelming advantage of position.

At the foot of the slope Jim turned left a little, then swung from the saddle to take his place in the line. Spaced out, they went up to the rim again on foot.

Some twenty feet away, Lars Johanssen showed a face flaming with enthusiasm in the clear, growing, shadowless light. "By Gom," he called, his face split in a big grin. "That Silver, he is von man!"

Jim grinned back, then stuck his head cautiously over the rim. In front of him, about two yards away, lay the sprawled body of a Mexican. Others were distributed along the rim, dead or wounded.

Beyond, down the gentle slope, there was a hundred yards of clear ground, then sparse brush, and the lifting bulk of a high, barren cliff.

Jim could hear a ranting, furious voice going down there in Spanish, and then, a little later, when he lifted his head incautiously, a bullet snarled past his ear.

He got his head down in a hurry. The range was too great for Colt-fire, so he could make no reply. A moment later, somebody passed a rifle up to him, with a box of cartridges, and he felt better. Now, he could be something more than a helpless target.

He took his hat off, stuck it on the end of his rifle and lifted it slowly. A bullet snapped through it and another whined overhead. He raised up swiftly, Winchester leveled.

From the brush below, two puffs of smoke drifted upward. Under one, he saw a slight movement, and squeezed the trigger. There was a sudden jerk in the bushes. The second rifle fired again, kicking up dust three inches in front of his ear. He levered, sighted and shot again.

Around him, other rifles were going, and from the bushes below a constant crackle of fire sounded, sending a scythelike sweep of lead toward the rim.

To his right, a Trent man half-stood, then rolled backward down the slope and lay still. Another grunted and lay forward, groaning, until the man next to him crawled over and pulled him down under cover.

BELOW, JIM saw Doc Brimstone, his beefy face drawn and yellow-colored now, working over the wounded.

Time passed, the minutes drawing long while the sun rode up the sky to shed a growing heat down on backs and shoulders.

To the right, Lars lifted up, with his usual attitude of believing that a mere bullet couldn't hurt him. He let out an exclamation of surprise.

"Hey, I tank dose fools are goin' to charge!" he called out.

Jim raised up for a look, and cursed wonderingly. Lars was right. The Mexicans below had led their horses up under cover. Now, apparently, they were forming an extended line back of the brush. He could hear horses trampling and see movement all along the line. The charging riders would take some bad punishment, but most of them would make it. Then it would be a close-quarters scrap against deadly odds.

Jim Clane's lips flattened and his blue eyes narrowed grimly.

"Looks like the finish," he muttered. "Well, we'll make 'em pay plenty."

He thought of Dave Dennison, wondered if Magpie and the others had managed to get him out. The sun had been up a long time, and, almost without his thinking about it, his hope had gotten lower and lower as the hot disk of flaming brass rode higher and higher. Now, he figured, he was liable never to know....

Trent slapped a shot out in answer to the lead that came from the flanks of the brush. Then, with a sudden yell, the charge burst into sight—more than half a hundred men thundering across the open space, rifles and sixguns spitting a storm of bullets.

Calm and fast, Jim drew a bead and squeezed the trigger. The Mexican he shot at reeled in the saddle and pitched off. Levering with all speed, he saw the line of horsemen check and waver, halfway. Half a dozen horses were down, kicking and squealing.

Others, with emptied saddles were racing off toward the flanks, colliding with those coming on.

He slammed lead again into that screaming confusion, scarcely able to see his target for the dust and smoke which steamed up from the mêlée. For an instant, it looked as though the charge might be broken.

Then a lean figure in fancy *vaquero's* clothes bellowed an order in Spanish, and the riders were coming on again.

A high-pitched rebel yell sounded from somewhere behind. It was answered by a shout of triumph from along the rim, but Jim paid no attention. A savage-eyed snarling rider was bearing down on him. The charge was up to the rim! He dropped his rifle, flashed up his sixguns and drove deadly slugs at that hurtling figure.

One of his bullets must have taken the horse in the forehead, for he checked and then slammed to the ground, sliding to within a yard of where Jim stood. The rider fell with his leg caught underneath his mount, but he did not know that, for he was dead before he hit the ground.

At Jim's side, Silver Trent's voice clarioned out, "After them. Run 'em to hell!"

As he spoke, his big, lean figure leapt forward, swift and supple and deadly, like a mountain lion charging.

JIM STARED, his jaw dropping. The attackers had broken. They had whirled their horses and were racing for the cover of the left-hand ravine. Then he saw the reason. A group of six or seven mounted men led by old Magpie Myers had broken out of the right-hand arroyo and were taking the Mexicans in the rear.

Guns roaring, mouths open in that fierce, high-pitched yell, they came racing in like a tornado.

Suddenly Jim gave a great shout, and in that moment his last doubt slid from him. Dave Dennison was there!

Jim leapt forward, his guns hammering a death's tattoo at the fleeing attackers. With the others, he chased them until they raced out of sight into the ravine. He checked at Silver's shouted command.

Somebody from the rim brought up horses and the Trent crowd flung itself into the saddle. The disorganized enemy had not stopped to make a stand, however. They had kept going at top speed. After a little, Silver called off the pursuit.

It was a jubilant crowd that galloped back to the basin and dismounted—jubilant, except for Silver Trent. His hawklike face was grim as he looked on his dead and wounded. And except for Magpie Myers, whose wrinkled, ageless face was drawn with worry.

"By God, Varro will pay me for this," Silver snapped through a tight throat.

Magpie Myers said gruffly, "Silver, I—I got some bad news."

"Yes?" Silver Trent's eyes were suddenly quiet, alert.

"They—they got Padre Pete an'—an' Gracia—Gracia Cortez...." The oldster's voice shook a little.

Silver Trent stood stock still, the color draining from his face.

"Who—what—?" Jim Clane would not have believed that anything could have made this man stammer like that.

Magpie Myers spread his hands. "Varro, I reckon," he said.

49

"A bunch raided the house last night—took both of 'em away. Left Juan with a message for you. He wouldn't tell it to me...."

Silver Trent whirled on Jim Clane, his eyes blazing with sudden fury. The impact of his glance shocked Jim like a blow, made him flinch a little, involuntarily. Trent's hands flashed out and closed around his throat.

"This is your fault, you pig-headed fool!" he blazed. His features were shaking with rage, but the grip of his hands was like crushing steel.

Jim fought against them in sudden desperation, but he might just as well have tried to loosen a shrinking collar of iron. Belatedly, his hands stabbed for his guns, but his head was already swimming, a red haze before his protruding eyes, and he groped for the Colt handles vainly. Silver Trent's eyes flaming into his own were made of pure murder.

Abruptly, the grip released. Jim staggered backward, gasping for air, his hands clawing feebly at his throat.

Silver passed a shaking hand over his forehead. "I—I'm sorry, Jim," he said. "I—I lost control of myself...."

Magpie Myers was staring at him open-mouthed. It was plain that he had never before seen Silver Trent out of hand.

Jim gulped, got his breath through a throat that throbbed with agony. Anger flared up in him, then died down as he took a look at Silver Trent's face. His lips were white, bloodless. The lines running down from his nose to the corners of his mouth were deep trenches, pain-drawn. And there was pain and fear in the depths of eyes, grown bleak and tragic as gray rocks in a storm.

Yet as he watched, Silver Trent straightened, and it was possible to see the strength flow back into him and the iron self-control clamp down again.

"Varro's smarter than I thought," he said evenly. "I didn't think he knew that Gracia meant anything to me."

"Might of jest took a chance," Magpie muttered. "Likely he ain't aimin' to—"

Silver was no longer listening. "Beau! Beau Buchanan!" he rapped out.

CHAPTER 7
OUTLAWS

A N IMMACULATELY clothed, dark, slender man came over. He was the man who had been drinking with Doc Brimstone the night before.

Jim had noticed him during the charge on the rim and later. He was one of those who had come up from behind Jim, and while Jim had not had time to think about it then, the sight of him had stayed in his mind—for this Beau Buchanan had managed to look as immaculate during the fight as before and after.

He was dressed in the black broadcloth of a gambler, with the tops of his trousers tucked into fine, hand-tooled boots, soft and newly polished. His manner during action had been as suave and cool as though that dog-fight had been a church sociable.

"I'm takin' Paolo and Magpie an' most of the rest an' ridin' into town," Silver Trent told him crisply. "You'll be in charge here. I don't reckon that crowd'll show up again, but keep a couple of scouts out, an' begin movin' up to the hideout if they do. Through slot canyon, it'll be easy to hold them off. The men that are wounded bad can be carried in stretchers."

Beau Buchanan permitted himself to look mildly surprised. "To town—by daylight?" he asked, with the implication that he thought it scarcely wise.

"Varro's got Padre Pete an' Gracia," Silver monotoned.

Beau Buchanan's lips tightened, then he spread his hands in a casual gesture. "If you'd let me come—"

Except for the icy hardness in his eyes Jim might have thought him unmoved.

Silver shook his head. "I need you here."

Magpie Myers was looking grave. His lips stirred, as though he were about to make some protest. Then he evidently thought better of it. It was plain that these men were not in the habit of questioning Silver Trent's judgment or orders.

Yet even Jim Clane could see that this move smacked of madness. They had escaped from that town by the skin of their teeth, at night. And it had brought some four score armed and deadly men on their trail. These men had just been fought off and were, presumably, on their way back to town. Now Silver Trent proposed to stick his head into that hornet's nest again by daylight, with fewer men—and with not only the survivors of the attack against him but the rest of the town as well. Especially, the *soldados* from whom Magpie had taken Dave Dennison!

Silver looked speculatively at Magpie Myers. "You figure it's suicide, don't you?" he asked softly.

52

Magpie stirred uncomfortably.

Abruptly, Silver turned away from him. "Men," he called out. His voice did not seem to lift much, yet every head snapped toward him instantly.

"Varro's taken Padre Pete and the Señorita Gracia," he said. "Somebody's got to go in an' find out what there is to be found out. Yet going in is a tough assignment. We may be wiped out. How many of you will volunteer to come, now, by daylight. Anyone who will, please step forward."

There was an instant of motionless silence, during which Jim could not decide whether the crowd was too shocked by the news to take it in all at once, or merely surprised at being asked if they would volunteer. Then a sort of universal snarl went up and the group moved as though jerked by one string—forward!

Jim saw Lars there, and hastily put himself in with the group His pulses were suddenly beating faster and his shoulders lifted. It came to him all at once that he was one of this crowd now, and a quick pride stirred in him. Outlaws? There was nothing in this raid for them. They were asked to face impossible odds merely for the sake of a priest and a girl. Yet not a man of them hesitated. Not a man but was chafing visibly to get into the saddle and ride!

Outlaws? Low laughter bubbled out of Jim Clane's throat. Yesterday, he thought, I'd have considered myself too good for them. Today....

He met Lar's dancing gaze and grinned.

Five minutes later, they were in the saddle.

ON THE way in, Dave Dennison told him what had

happened. He had been taken out at daybreak from his cell, with his hands tied behind him, and stood up against the wall of the prison. He had asked not to have his eyes covered, so he had been able to see what had happened.

There had been a sudden disturbance at the gate, a guard had gone down, then another, so fast and so silently that the squad in front of Dave had hardly noticed it. Then a barked command, and Dave had seen that the walls were lined with Winchesters.

Actually, there had only been four of them, and two men at the gate, but it looked to Dave, and to the *soldados*, like an army. They had taken him out without firing a shot.

"Durn if I blamed them greasers, either," Dave grinned. "This crowd shore looked like business. An' the thing was so quiet and shore an' fast." His face sobered, looked a little embarrassed. "I'm kind of obliged to all you boys," he said.

Jim snorted. "What we had to do with it was nothin', exactly."

Dave Dennison shook his head. "I've heard all about it," he said quietly. "An' I'm obliged."

"Who the hell is this Varro?" Jim asked, to change the subject.

"You don't know? Didn't Trent tell you?"

"I reckon he would have," Jim said wryly, "only I was bein' kind of bull-headed."

"I learned it in jail," Dave said grimly. "One of the other prisoners talked to me finally last night. I reckon he figured he was spillin' to a dead man so it was all right. Varro's a big rancher—*haciendero*—aroun' here. *Don Esteban Varro y Queyan* is his full handle. But he's more than that. He runs a bunch of *bandidos* that think about as much of murder as you an' me do of brandin' a calf. The Mex call him *El Diablo* when they think nobody's listenin', but they don't do much talkin' about him at all.

"Mostly they'll just go gray-yeller an' cross theirself if you start talkin' about him. I don't know just how he got 'em that way, but they're plumb scared to death of him. He's the big auger behind them raids we been gettin' up above the border. First, I figured it was Silver Trent, but I found out different. Then, all of a sudden, I was in jail, charged with killin' a corpse I hadn't ever seen. The prisoner that talked let it out that Varro was the man that had me framed. Seems I was askin' too many questions about him. It was knowed, too, that you was on your way in, an' that Varro meant to put a couple of slugs in you. It was his crowd that jumped you all out at the camp. Him an' Silver Trent has been tanglin'—I don't know just how or why."

Jim's mouth flattened into a grim line across his face. So that was the explanation of the scrap in the cantina. This Varro had just been having them murdered, was all! And if it hadn't been for Silver Trent, he probably would have succeeded. Not only that, but El Diablo was to be thanked for drygulching their two partners with the herd and getting himself and Lars outlawed. Quite a little score to be settled!

So his thoughts ran, ironic, bitter, full of hatred, until the spraddle of adobe buildings, which was Sangre, appeared in the valley below.

Jim's chest tightened a little then, and his nerves crisped. For Silver Trent was leading them straight across the open, moving at a steady trot, without haste and without hesitation. Then they were at the edge of town, riding down the main street!

55

A man looked out of a window at them, stared, motionless, his face frozen into an expression of alarmed astonishment At a corner ahead, a *soldado* came to an open-mouthed halt, made a movement as though he were going to run and spread the alarm, then thought better of it and hastily assumed an expression of indifference. From a doorway, a woman called excitedly to someone inside.

Jim Clane looked ahead at the cavalcade, for the first time seeing closely and by daylight these men with whom he rode. There were no more than fifteen or sixteen with himself and Lars and Dave. Except for Silver and Magpie and one other, they were all Mexicans. But they were Mexicans of a kind Jim Clane had not previously known. Bigger men, most of them, than the average below the Border, with a scornful pride in the flash of dark eyes and the set of fierce mouths. Swaggerers. Buckaroos of the Borders. Aristocracy. Magnificent now in their calm disdain for the death which might blast at them from any corner.

They made a sight to lift a man's heart, riding at a walk now, every man jack of them superbly mounted and looking as though he had been born in a saddle. No tension in the easy, arrogant set of those shoulders. Relaxed, yet with a deadly readiness instinct somehow in the very casualness of them. Fighting men, these, who plainly loved nothing quite so much as the bright face of danger—not even the dark eyes of the señoritas that looked out at them, half admiring and half afraid, from windows and doorways.

CHAPTER 8
KILLER'S RENDEZVOUS

FROM AN alleyway ahead, a girl of fifteen emerged, the sweet curves of maturity already swelling through her child's slenderness. She walked with the swaying-hipped grace of one already sure of herself and her beauty.

Her eyes fell on the column and its leader. The color drained from her face and her dark eyes were suddenly wide and frightened.

"*El Halcon de la Sierra!*" she gasped.

Silver Trent's smile was swift and queerly tender. "Have no fear, Chiquita," he teased. "The great hawks do not prey on doves."

The color flooded back into the girl's face, but now she remained speechless until Trent had ridden by her.

A Mexican in the line behind swept off his sombrero and leaned forward with assumed ferocity, "Yet the lesser hawks do, my beautiful pigeon," he said. "Guard yourself well, lest I make a morsel of you!"

The girl tossed her head. "Does the crow caw when the falcon's wings are spread?" she demanded pertly.

Delighted laughter ran through the column, in which the outlaw who had been bested joined as heartily as anybody else.

Muted laughter ran along the windows, too—laughter that had a suddenly friendly ring, so that Jim Clane narrowed his eyes thoughtfully. There might come a time, he guessed, when this Silver Trent, who, it now appeared, was called the Hawk of the Sierra, might ride into this town without too much danger.

Later, he said as much to Ricardo Juarez, who rode beside him. The man threw back his head and laughed.

"Amigo," he said, "you begin to see some things, but you have yet much to learn. This town is still strange to us. One day, you will see the people run into the streets to kneel to Silver Trent as he passes."

Jim tossed him a doubting glance, but did not answer. His attention had become riveted on a man in the street ahead, who was staring open-mouthed, yet with fury in his face also. There was something familiar about that figure—those fancy *vaquero's* clothes, that wiry leanness. Then he got it. It was the man who had led that last charge out at camp!

"Hey! That's—"Jim's hands blurred toward his guns. Ricardo put a quick, restraining hand on his arm.

"Silver knows," he said quietly.

The lean *vaquero* ahead had been standing half-crouched, his hands clawed a little, as though he were about to go for his guns. Now he straightened, vanished like a shadow into the doorway beside him.

"But hell," Jim protested. "That's the man who caused us all all the trouble—killed some of your partners. He'll bring that whole gang down on us."

Ricardo shrugged. "Perhaps," he said quietly. "But Silver does not shoot men down on the street—not when the odds are sixteen to one."

Jim Clane felt the color start hot at his collar-line and surge upward in a burning flood. His reaction had been instinctive—unthought-out—because he had been taken by surprise. He realized now that he himself would not have shot without warning, or without waiting for the other man to draw. But he could not say so. It would sound like an afterthought—an excuse.

He swung eyes gone suddenly cold on Ricardo. "In the future, when I go for my guns or do anything else, keep your hands off me, hombre, unless you're looking for trouble," he hummed. "Do you understand?"

Ricardo lifted an apologetic hand, and his teeth flashed suddenly in a warm and friendly smile.

"You are right in what you say, *amigo*," he said. "I did not have time to think. And I know what I did was not necessary with you."

Jim Clane stared at him for a moment, then he drew a deep breath and grinned wryly.

"You said a little while ago that I still had a lot to learn," he said. "I reckon you were right."

The cavalcade turned abruptly off into an alley which Jim vaguely recognized. He swung into it, frowning abstractedly as he studied it.

"Look here," he said abruptly to Ricardo, "Silver says he left that gun by the fire for me on purpose. Do you believe that?" He eyed the Mexican closely, watching his expression.

Ricardo smiled. "It was that which I had forgotten," he said. Then, as an afterthought, "It's a trick of his. It is his way to gamble. He will not have a bad killer ride with him. Sometimes a good fighter will kill in the back, or shoot when the other man

is not ready. Silver must find out. He thinks he knows already, eh? Because he knows men. But he must find out. So he puts his life up for the bet, and then he knows. He is sure." He shrugged, tossing out a palm in a gesture of complete carelessness.

"I think he enjoys this gambling. Eh?" he went on. "But also, it is useful. You were very angry. Will you lose your head and do murder? But this is also a great compliment, *amigo mio*. It is

Silver Trent moved like a
striking mountain cat.

because he has already chosen you except for that. He has seen
you and judged you and he will let you ride with him. There are
men who would give their right arms for that."

Jim Clane looked at him, a little stunned. He could see the
deep fierce pride running in this man because he also was a Trent
man. He had been chosen. Despite himself, something in Jim
responded, setting a queer, lifting thrill under his breastbone

that he had never felt the like of before. It was a new experience to him.

In a way, it was a laugh. Proud of being chosen to be an outlaw! Then he remembered soberly that he already was an outlaw, and would remain one until he could find this Mex Varro and choke the truth out of him.

THE CAVALCADE drew up before a walled house which Jim recognized at once. Most of the men stayed in the saddle, but Silver swung down with Magpie and Paolo and went into the house.

Jim hesitated, then got out of the saddle also, tossing his reins to Dave Dennison. He hadn't been invited in, but Silver had said that this thing was his—Jim's—fault, and he meant to be in on it all the way through.

He set his jaw against a possible bawling out and went in, feeling himself getting sore because he knew that he was already a little afraid of Silver Trent's disapproval. It was a relief, somehow, to find Lars Johanssen's big form alongside at his elbow.

Inside the dim house, furnished with the deeply carven furniture of old Spain, Silver Trent was talking to Juan, the servant. Juan's head was bandaged, as though he had been hit on it, and his face was drawn, lined with grief and anxiety.

"…They came quickly—a dozen of them. The padre was here, in this room, reading his breviary. Señorita Gracia sat sewing. They brushed past me, rushed inside. They seized the Señorita and the Padre—I swear to you that I would not have believed this sacrilege if I had not seen it with these eyes. I fought, Señor—but one hit me from behind, on the head…."

Silver Trent stirred a little, the small movement of his muscles charged with a ravening impatience.

"The message," he interrupted sharply. "Who did this thing?"

"It is a trap, Señor—the message." Juan spoke heavily. "A trap of—" He crossed himself hurriedly and was silent

"El Diablo?" Silver Trent's voice was harsh, strained.

Juan nodded dumbly. His face had lost color.

"When I came to," he went on, his voice lowered, "there were two who had remained. One—a man of as evil a face as I have ever looked on—said, 'Say this to Silver Trent, and to no other: He is to come alone, or with no more than two of his men, to—where he knows. There is one who wishes an understanding with him. The road will be watched. If there are more than Trent and two others, or if others try to follow, then the girl and the priest will never be seen again. If Trent comes, they will be freed, unharmed.' That was all, Señor."

Silver stood with the muscles of his jaws ridged out like whitened steel. His big, shapely, powerful hands opened and closed, clenching on the air as on an enemy's throat.

He whispered through set teeth, "He knew then! Somehow, he knew! He is well-named, this devil. But, by God, this time he'll find he's caught a bobcat not so easy to singe!"

Paolo had been listening with the white anger of fanaticism glowing in his long, lean, highbrowed face. He swung on Silver Trent.

"Give me but half an hour and I can raise fifty, a hundred men in this town. We'll leave no single dog of them alive. We'll raid and burn and plunder and kill until we are glutted with it, so that this thing shall not be unavenged!"

Silver laughed without mirth. "And leave the Padre and Gracia to be killed? Varro means what he says."

Paolo's face blazed. "What else is there to do? Besides, God will take care of his own. Is it not always that way?"

Silver shook his head, almost absently. "Take the men back to the camp, Magpie," he said curtly. "I'm ridin' up to Varro's place."

Magpie stared. "Alone? You gone loco?"

"It's the only chance we've got."

"You know how long you'll live, don't you?"

"That's to be seen."

"An' do you think he'll let the girl and Padre Pete off, jest because you come? You ain't thinkin', Silver."

Silver Trent's face was white and strained. "No," he said quietly, "I don't believe he'll let them go. But I also know that if we try to go up there with more than three men, he'll kill them at once. Their only chance is for me to go. Maybe, when I'm there I can find a way...."

"No! No! This is a madness," Paolo burst out. "You are playing his game. This is what he wanted you to do. Of what use to seek certain death for yourself when you cannot aid those he already has?"

Silver's lips were a solid, sombre line, implacable and unswerving. "Yet I am going," he said quietly.

Paolo drew himself up. "Ver' good," he said, breaking into English. "Then, I, Paolo, go also."

Trent shook his head. "No."

"Hell, you don't think you're ridin' into somethin' like that without us?" Magpie sounded outraged. "You're gittin' soft in the head. He said you could take two men. We're ridin' with you."

Silver lost the remote, abstracted look. His eyes warmed as he put a hand on each of the men's shoulders.

"That's why he said I could bring two men," he said, a little grimly. "So he'd get everybody at the head of the outfit on one deal. He figured that you would be the two to come with me. Or hoped for it. But we'll be too smart for him there. I need you two to stay with the gang."

"But that don't go for me," Jim Clane broke in savagely. "You said I was to blame for this, so I'm in it—an' stayin' in it to the finish."

"Yah," Lars seconded him stubbornly. "Me, too. Ve ride vit'. I ban have somethin' to say vit' dis Diablo dot he vill not forget even in Hell."

The grimness around Silver's lips tightened. For a moment he seemed to hesitate, then abruptly he said, "All right. You ride with me—both of you."

His eyes were warm.

CHAPTER 9
INTO THE TRAP

ONCE HIS decision was taken, Silver wasted no time. Within five minutes the three of them were on the trail toward the badlands south of Sangre, beyond which lay the great, broken, grassy hills and valleys which formed the cattle domain of Don Esteban Varro.

By that time, Silver was already regretting having allowed Jim and Lars to come with him He knew that he was facing his greatest danger. He was giving himself freely into the hands of an enemy who had neither conscience nor honor nor mercy— whose word was to be less trusted than a friendly overture from a diamondback rattler. He was going, unless his own quick thinking and readiness could somehow get him out of it, to certain death—and a vain and useless death in the bargain. For his dying would do nothing to save Gracia Cortez and Padre Pete.

And as certainly as he, Silver Trent, died, so also would Jim and Lars die.

He had taken them along because he guessed that if he had not done so they would have followed anyhow. Jim Clane was stubborn and hot-headed enough for it. And that would have been worse for them. Perhaps also worse for the priest and the girl. There was no alternative.

Then he put the regret out of his mind, and turned his thoughts to the practical business ahead of him. Nothing could be gained by thinking of possible consequences. And Silver was not the kind to admit defeat before it came. Somehow, he had to accomplish his ends, find a way to outwit Varro's diabolic intelligence.

The shock of learning that Garcia and the Padre had been taken, with the full realization of the fate in store for them, had begun to wear off now. His faculties began to work with their old ease and swift clarity.

Varro, having won this trick so neatly, would in all likelihood be overconfident, and that was always a bad thing to be with Silver Trent. He would, he guessed, be allowed to ride unmolested most of the way. Then he would be met by a party of Varro's riders who would disarm him and take him into the *haciendero's* presence. He had no fear of being killed beforehand. El Diablo would scarcely forego the pleasure of seeing him die, slowly and unpleasantly.

Suddenly, he laughed a little, softly. Yes, there would be chances—chances created by this man's overweening conceit and ravening cruelty. His mind began to play with possibilities, began to foresee the things that might happen. It was Silver Trent's way....

Yet in one thing he was wrong. Don Esteban Varro, whom men called El Diablo, was not so overconfident as he might have been. He had a shrewder estimate of his enemy than Silver believed.

Things had not gone as well as he had expected. The news had already reached him of the defeat he had suffered in the fight at the camp, and a poisonous anger rode him. Failure, even temporary failure, was anathema to this man, and there was in him, deep under his cold shrewdness, something superstitious which whispered to him that there was ill luck somehow in this war with Silver Trent.

He scowled under the shadow of his black gold-embroidered sombrero, and drove his stick viciously into the gravel of the path on which he walked. Standing so, lost in venomous thought, his misshapen form hunched in the dark folds of a long cape, he looked infinitely evil, a creature ascended from some nether region, loathing the sunlight and men who walked under the sun.

A stray hound that still had some of the eagerness and touching faith of a puppy in him, sensed the evilness of this spirit a little too late. He came bounding out of the hacienda garden, ears cocked and tail wagging playfully. His wiggling enthusiasm and friendliness carried him to within a yard of Esteban Varro before he stopped, the change in his attitude comic in its suddenness.

Varro's hand moved with almost unbelievable swiftness. The heavy stick he carried keened through the air in a barely visible arc. It struck the dog over the back, as, desperately and too late, the animal attempted to flee. It cracked his spinal column just forward of his hind quarters.

The animal gave one agonized yelp, then broke into the frantic, half-human yapping of a dog that has been badly hurt. Desperately, he clawed himself off into the bushes, his hind-quarters dragging, his anguished voice filling the sunlit air with its pleading clamor.

ESTEBAN VARRO stood hunched and motionless, a faint, cruel smile wreathing his lips. A peon came running, saw the dark, cloaked figure on the path and stopped abruptly, with an obsequious bow.

Varro turned eyes on him which were like the points of a frozen drill.

"Well?" he demanded coldly. "You want something?"

"Excuse me, Señor, no," the peon stammered, fear plain in him. "The dog—I did not know what was the matter...."

"Then get back to your work, fool, lest there be another dog with his back broken."

The peon breathed, "Si, Señor," and hurried away.

Varro's smile deepened for a moment. Then he continued his leisurely way up the path. Behind him, the agony of the dog still made the day hideous. It did not bother Varro. He knew that the peon would spread the word and that no one else would dare come now, with stupid, sentimental hands, to put the animal out of his misery.

At the steps of the veranda a man was waiting. He bowed humbly to Varro. The *haciendero* halted, flicking him a glance of wicked appraisal.

"You are Carlos Figuero?"

The other man bowed. "Si, Señor."

He was a straight-shouldered Mexican, garbed as a small cattleman, with a firm, agreeable face which just now looked vaguely worried.

"Come in," Varro told him curtly.

He led the way into the living room which was furnished in gloomy splendor, and seated himself behind an ornate desk in one corner, leaving the other man standing.

"Ten years ago," Varro said softly, "you escaped from the prison at Juarez."

Carlos Figuero gasped, his eyes suddenly panicky.

"You had served one of a ten year term for robbery," Varro

went on in that soft, relentless voice. "If you were taken back, it would be for a longer time."

Carlos Figuero's hands were knotted before him, and a vein stood out suddenly in his forehead.

"I—Señor—" he stammered pleadingly. "I was not guilty. Please, I beg of you…."

"You were convicted," Varro told him evenly. "That is enough. But perhaps you may not have to go back."

"Señor—anything…."

Esteban Varro looked at him through narrowed eyes. "You worked once in the silver mines at Monte Hijo," he said significantly. "Your record there was good. You could go back. You captained the bullion train. You could do so again, and you could lead it off the trail, to a place I picked out."

Carlos Figuero's face had gone gray. "Señor—" his voice was pleading, desperate—"I have gone straight for ten long years. I am married. I have a little son. Show mercy. I can't—"

"Can't go back to jail?" Varro interrupted, sneering. "But you can, my friend. I have only to notify the Rurales. Then you will go. And what will happen to your wife while you are gone? I think my men might like to see her. She is not bad looking, no?"

Figuero caught his breath, and for a moment his eyes held pure murder.

"I—you—" he ground out, and took a step toward the desk, with his hands clawed into hooks.

A sixgun looked at him suddenly.

"You forget yourself a little," Varro said softly.

Carlos Figuero brought up sharp. For a moment he stood tense, rigid, then his shoulders slumped.

"I will do as you wish, Señor," he said brokenly.

Varro's smile was cruel. He put the sixgun on the desk before him.

"That is a little more sensible," he said dryly. "But you need not feel so sad about it, hombre. My men are well-paid. You will be better off than you are on that little piece of over-grazed ranch of yours. Go, and report here this evening. You'll have a little ride, to help you get back into the way of things."

Galloping hoofs sounded outside, slid to a skidding halt before the veranda. Footsteps, half-running, sounded in the hall, and a moment later a thick-lipped, pockmarked Mexican burst in at the door.

"Master, he is coming—he and two others," he gasped out.

Varro motioned Carlos Figuero out and came to his feet, his eyes gleaming.

"Trent?"

"Si, Señor. *El Halcon*, and two others.

Varro's lips writhed into a snarl. *"El Halcon!* Witless son of a dog! What do you mean by calling him by a name like that. Don't let me hear another such buffoonery out of you!"

The messenger's mouth stiffened, as though fear had gone into him.

"Si, Señor—if the señor will excuse…."

"Stop babbling! Who are the others?"

"The two gringos who fought in the cantina, Señor."

El Diablo's face darkened in sudden fury. "Fool! Liar! They

must be Myers and Paolo. Why would he bring two clowns of cowboys?"

The pock-faced man's lips were still stiff, but the fear was not enough to make him cringe. His eyes were steady as he answered.

"I am not mistaken. I saw them with these eyes."

VARRO RECOVERED his temper as quickly as he had lost it. He sat for a moment in silence, pulling at his lower lip. "It was too much to hope that he would bring them," he said slowly, as though thinking aloud. "Still…." His eyes grew intent, concentrated. Then he shook his head, as though throwing off a minor disappointment and his lean dark face began to glow again.

His hands clawed in a fierce gesture before him. "No mistake must be made," he muttered. "Where is he now?"

"On the range near Cabeza Creek," the pock-faced man replied instantly. "That is where he was—about five miles from here, heading straight for the hacienda. I killed my horse getting here. He must be still three miles distant."

"Take six men—your best," Varro directed incisively. "Get Trent and his two men and disarm all three. Then tie their hands behind them. Take no chances. This Silver Trent is as dangerous as a cornered catamount. Get his arms first, so that he will not be able to object to being tied. He will submit rather than fight, Tell him that if shots are fired, the girl and the old man will be dead before he can get to this house."

"Si, Señor."

"You are sure that nobody is following him?"

"Certain, Señor. The trails have all been watched. I had signal smoke telling me that these three were coming long before they got onto our range. No others follow."

"Go then, but send me Black Juan here."

When the pock-faced man had gone, Varro began to pace the room feverishly. He walked with a limp because one leg was thinner and shorter than the other. His great shoulders were twisted and hunched. It gave him a dwarfish and deformed aspect, though it was obvious that except for whatever accident of birth or later life had made him as he was, he would have been a man of considerable size. His arms looked unusually large and hung almost to his knees. Hunched between his shoulders, his twisted head looked small, but the brow was wide and high, with something almost beautiful about it.

It was only the lower part of the face which looked cruel and evil, with a queer, degenerate baseness about it. Yet even so, the lean jaw, thrusting out under the thin, sharply hooked nose, had power, and the queerly flexible, nervous mouth held a thin-lipped strength as well as cruelty.

As he walked, he thumbed his lower lip and muttered unintelligibly to himself. His eyes were excited, blazing pools of hell.

Hatred controlled Esteban Varro's life—hatred and an inexhaustible cruelty. Hatred sharpened his wits and dictated his thoughts and formed the motivating force for his immense lust for power. But no other hatred in Varro's life compared to the hatred he bore Silver Trent. And Silver Trent was about to be delivered into his hands, bound and helpless!

As that thought grew in him, took the shape and form of

reality, he halted his pacing and his powerful, clawlike hands clutched at his throat, as though the triumph and ecstasy were too much for him to bear. He would see Silver Trent die. But before he died, he would no longer be a man, but only the broken, tortured, witless shell of one.

Varro's hands lifted, clawed and shaken, toward the ceiling, as though he were invoking some hideous, hidden god of loathing.

"A-ah!" he muttered. "If only I dared to keep him alive for years, so that I could see him suffer every hour of every day. Then—then my life would be worth the living!"

But he knew that he did not dare that. Silver Trent would be too hard to keep. Silver Trent might escape. And then Esteban Varro would walk in fear again. No, Trent had to die—all too quickly. Only so, could El Diablo be sure of keeping his life and holding the power for evil which was more precious to him than life itself.

Waiting for Black Juan, he stood chafing by the window, looking out. Suddenly his breath went in with a sound like a low, tremulous whistle. Between the cottonwoods which made a windbreak in front of the hacienda, across half a mile of level range in front, a party of nine men had come in sight. They were riding at a gallop toward the house. Three of them were astride horses which were being led by three of the others!

Silver Trent had been caught! It had really happened, in just the way Varro had planned it. Until now he had not been able really to make himself believe that the thing would come off. But it was so. His vengeance was at hand!

CHAPTER 10
FACE TO FACE

CANTERING TOWARDS the house, Silver Trent's brain was busy, and his eyes alert. This was the first time that he had come to the Hacienda de Varro, but his mental picture of it was already clearer and more detailed than would have been that of the ordinary man after half a dozen visits.

They had come unmolested through the badlands which bordered the plateau, and which formed a natural defense for Varro's realm. At the back of the badlands, the rimrock rose sheer, cut only by one deep ravine, which ran up to the plateau.

The plateau itself was surrounded by mountains on all sides, and formed a great basin through which two streams ran. There was grazing here for ten thousand head of cattle.

Some five miles from the badlands end of the basin was the hacienda itself. Approaching it, Silver saw that it was a great, gray pile of stone which looked like a medieval castle. In a country where the architecture was flat-roofed, low, and of adobe construction, it was a surprising sight.

Back of it, rose a high, sheer cliff, and between this wall of rock and the hacienda was a ravine down which rushed one of the two streams which watered the plateau.

In front, and at the sides, were gardens, beautifully laid out and carefully tended. To the left, at some distance, were auxiliary buildings and two large corrals, in which a couple of hundred horses milled. The buildings themselves looked almost like a small village, and it was evident that they housed the *vaqueros* and ranch hands.

Silver knew that this man Varro kept nearly a hundred men as permanent hands, at the hacienda, and that he had as many more on his payroll, scattered about the countryside below.

This latter hundred was almost like an army of occupancy in conquered territory. Esteban Varro's power had spread, as a plague spreads, from one center, until it appeared that there would be no end to it. In towns like Sangre, the local government officials were his paid men, and aided him in levying toll throughout a countryside which had been taught to live in terror of his name.

It was this latter fact which had given Silver Trent the measure of the man and made him his enemy.... For Silver had seen Varro's brand of terror at its worst.

By strange chance he had seen Varro kill his partner, and throw his partner's young wife—whom he intended to steal—into a burning building, when she refused to yield to his lust.

Silver had left Varro for dead then, but somehow, miraculously, that tyrant had survived his lead. Since that time, on several occasions, the paths of the two had crossed, though they had never met again in person, and each time Silver Trent had managed to score a minor victory. Now Varro had seized Gracia Cortez, daughter of that same woman he had cast into the flames....

Because of his knowledge of Varro's methods, Silver knew it would require the utmost in strategy to break his power. He had been a long ways from ready for a showdown when Jim Clane

"It is a pity that these poor devils have not the keys, either to
the door or to your chains," he said tauntingly.

and Lars Johanssen had turned up and gotten into a jam which had forced his hand. Even then, he had hoped to withdraw and gather his strength before he really went up against El Diablo. For that, he needed more men—at least twice as many as he had—and he needed time, for he could not devote every day to a war with Varro. There was much else to be done.

His own men had to be fed and rewarded. Men who lived by outlawry had to give their attention to it. And the fact that Silver Trent's brand of outlawry was unique made another difficulty: for the Trent gang did not prey on the poor, or even on the decent rich. It was only from the crooked and oppressive among the men of wealth, on both sides of the border, that El Halcon de la Sierra collected toll. That meant hard riding, and far riding, and greater risk. It also required men of a certain caliber—men that could not be picked up at every crossroads of outlawry.

So Silver had hoped to bide his time and avoid open war until he was ready. But the shrewdness and devilish ingenuity of Esteban Varro had made that impossible. Even now, Silver could not guess how Varro had managed to hit on his one weak spot—how he had guessed that Gracia was the one thing he would fight harder for and endure more for than anything in the world. Only Padre Pete knew that secret, and it was not possible that the Padre talked. Not even the girl, Gracia, knew….

In a moment, he might learn how it was that Varro had guessed. At any rate, he would come face to face with the man whose deeds had aroused such loathing in him. It was a pity that he had to come as a prisoner, with his hands bound behind him and all the cards in Varro's hands. Perhaps some time there would be a different story.

THE SHADOWS of a smile crossed Silver's strong lips, and for a moment his fingers curled at his belt, behind his back. Not quite all the cards were in Varro's hand. One, and an ace, was sewn into that belt: a slender, razor sharp sliver of steel, which would cut through the ropes that bound Silver's hands as though they were butter.

It was probable that he could work free of his bonds in any case, but perhaps not fast enough for his purposes. Silver Trent was a hard man to tie, because of the supple cords of muscles around his wrists. Hardened, they stood out like iron against the tightening ropes. Relaxed, they left the bonds loose, made it possible to work free of them.

But that took a little time, and Silver had a hunch that when the moment came he'd be in a hurry. Esteban Varro would give him few chances, make very few, if any, mistakes.

In front of the house, the Mexicans who had "captured" them—to Jim Clane's obvious disgust it had been a peaceable surrender—dismounted, and the leader motioned to Silver and the others to do likewise.

The Mexicans had ridden with their guns drawn and ready. They relaxed none of their vigilance now. The leader preceded them up the garden walk, the three prisoners following in single file, with two guards on either side of them and one bringing up the rear. They were very careful.

At the porch, the leader halted them, and went into the house alone. He returned in a moment and motioned the three prisoners inside, telling the guards to wait.

Silver led the way, following the pockmarked man down a gloomy, magnificent hallway, and into the room where El Diablo waited, a dark, hunched figure behind his great, carven desk.

In the middle of the huge room, Silver halted, something like surprise and shock inside him, even though he had expected this, been sure to find it. Yet it seemed strange somehow, and impossible—even uncanny.

"So it's you, is it?" he said slowly. "I thought it would be."

The man who called himself Esteban Varro bared his teeth in a triumphant sneer.

"Me! Yes! Still recognizable, it seems—even though not quite the same!"

Silver's eyes narrowed. "Men don't change much—inside."

Varro's dark face was almost luminescent in the fire of pure hatred that burned behind it. He slapped his hands suddenly onto the desk, pushing himself to his feet, as though the drive of emotion in him had sent a galvanizing thrust through his muscles, independent of his will. He circled the desk, walked out into Silver's view.

"But not quite the same outside!" he snarled. "A hip that won't work. A leg shriveled, half-paralyzed. A shoulder lower than the other. Back hunched over a smashed breastbone. The body distorted like the soul, eh?" He let out a high bark of laughter—laughter so alive with fury and hatred as to sound like the death-lusting cry of a maniac.

"Look on your work, Trent—Señor Trent—great ape of

80

Virtue! Congratulate yourself! Remember how you came roaring into what was none of your business and shot me to bloody doll rags? Ah-h! You felt fine didn't you? The first and the last time that anyone ever beat Esteban Varro! And it was you—great self-righteous zany. Your booming, God-bootlicking guns hammering their virtuous slugs into me." His clenched left fist hammered his chest, and again that high, maniacal laughter burst from his throat. "Into *me!* ME!"

The laughter died and he crept toward Silver, his face a contorted mask of pure hatred.

"You and I shall laugh together over it, my friend," he whispered. "We shall laugh while you die, my *dear* friend. For you are going to die very slowly, *amigo carrissimo.* I am going to twist and break those great bones of yours one by one. I—with these hands! But before you quite die, you are going to see things happen to the little girl, eh? Ah, yes. How we shall laugh over that! Dishonor worse than death, I think they call it in your great windy, empty, strutting world—*amigo mio!*"

Behind his back, Silver Trent's supple fingers moved suddenly.

He could feel the muscles in his throat and face go rigid with the effort to keep out expression, feel the great vein in his temple swell and pound.

He had not meant to try a break now. Some instinct warned him that this was not the time or place. He did not know enough yet, was not sure.... Yet, he knew with sudden, deadly certainty that it had better be quick. This raving, hating soul from hell meant what he said, had prepared, planned, only for this.

AT THE fringe of his vision, Silver could see the others, knew

81

that they understood also. Jim Clane's lean-muscled face had gone a little pale. A beading of sweat glistened on his fore-head. Lars Johanssen held his head down and forward, like a bull about to charge, but there was sudden fear even in him, for his tongue slid suddenly along dry lips. And Silver knew that against the evil, the dark, elemental horror here revealed, even these two could not quite defend themselves.

They were looking into the soul of Esteban Varro, and their eyes were fixed on what they saw with the ghastly fascination of men hypnotized by some supernatural, flesh-creeping thing.

"You will see her die, also. You will not say that the other was worse than death then," the ghastly whispering voice went on. "Have you ever heard a woman scream under torture? Scream and scream and scream until her mind breaks and she is an idiot—whimpering, babbling, ready to be slaughtered like sick beef? You will see it, and hear it, my friend—before your own mind cracks, and you go yelling mad. Before you beg like a groveling dog for the death that will release you. Ah-h! Death is too good—"

Silver Trent's short, calm laugh cut him off. "You're maun-dering, Gonzales," he said contemptuously. "Or Varro—which is it? I believe you really think you had the right to kill your partner and steal his wife—to slug her and toss her into a burn-ing building because she tried to claw your eyes out instead of yielding to your ardor. You feel abused because I happened along and shot you for the dog you are. It's a pity I left you for dead, without seeing to it that you were. Tell me, how did you know about—Gracia."

"I saw her!" Varro leaned forward and spat the words at him as a spitting cobra sprays venom. "When you hid out with these cow-clowns in the priest's house I went to have a look. Did you think I would not recognize her because she was only seven when I last saw her? You fool! She is like her mother. Ha-ha-hah! Like her I sent living to hell in the flames—beautiful like that the fire ate so no other could take it from me! Beautiful—this one, that I will have before your eyes and kill—kill so horribly that—"

Something snapped in Silver Trent. This man was still three paces from him and at the side, with a clear field of fire, the pock-marked Mexican stood with his gun naked in his hand and his mouth loose with the lust of cruelty. Yet the silver of steel bit through the ropes then, and Silver Trent moved, like a striking mountain-cat.

Esteban Varro loosed a startled squawk and tried to duck back, get clear of those swooping, steel-sinewed arms. From the right, where the pock-marked man stood beyond Jim and Lars, the sixgun blasted.

Lead howled past Silver's ears, touched like a swift and deadly feather at the back of his neck, leaving its mark of blood.

Then he had Varro in his hands and was swinging him for a shield against the next shot. But the devil in black was no longer trying to get away. There was stark fear in the evil depths of his eyes, but now he came at Silver, gripping with hands that had such strength as to send a shock of apprehension through the big outlaw's mind.

Those long arms caught around his arms, the hands gripping

behind his back, the distorted body clinging close. It was like being in the grip of some huge and evil spider.

Desperately, he lifted and swung, turning Varro's back to the pock-marked gunman in time to stop another shot. Straining, the piston muscles of his right arm forced upward, breaking the grip of one of El Diablo's hands, clasping steel fingers about the corded, laboring throat.

Murder was in Silver Trent's heart at that moment. The loathing in him for this evil-breathed, clinging thing could have no satisfaction except in crushing and killing. His hand closed hard against Varro's wind-pipe, the bruising fingers biting deep into flesh.

The pock-faced man was rushing toward him, gun in hand. Jim Clane's foot swung out, caught the Mexican's belly in a driving, toe-pointed kick. The gunman's breath went out explosively. He doubled and sank to the floor, groaning horribly.

Silver had scarcely a glance for him. His hand was closing Esteban Varro's windpipe. In a moment, the voice-box would break.

The man's breath was a strangled rattle: "Juan! Black…" Stark terror yammered in his eyes.

"Look out, Silver!" It was Lars' frantic call—Lars, with his hands behind his back, charging head-down like a bull.

Then something exploded in the back of Silver Trent's head. A blinding white light filled his brain, faded, with blackness rushing in its train. His knees buckled. He fought to keep from falling, tried to twist, but felt something stunning fall on his head again.

Consciousness, life, was seeping out of him. Agonized, his will clawed up in him, fought to beat the blackness. He turned, his powerful hands clutching blindly.

It was like the shattering impact of an axe, that third blow, then. His knees gave like loose cotton. There was nothing afterwards but the blackness.

CHAPTER 11
THE STONE CELL

SILVER FOUGHT his way up through the darkness. His head was a blinding throbbing agony. Half-seeing, half-conscious, he tried to raise a hand, felt metal jerk at his wrists. Handcuffs.

The realization of it shocked at once into full consciousness. He opened his eyes. He was in a room so dim that at first he thought his vision must be injured. But then he realized that it was twilight, and that through one barred window so little light came as to leave the room almost in darkness. He was sitting on a stone floor. Then he made out his companions, and memory came back to him altogether.

"You all right, Silver?" Lars' voice was anxious.

"Yes." Silver's reply was crisp. "Where are we?"

Instead of answering, Jim Clane shook his head. "Hombre," he said wonderingly, "you can sure take a hammering. What the hell you got aroun' that head of your'n anyway?"

Silver grinned faintly and put his hands to his head. They

came away wet and sticky, and there was dried blood on his face and neck.

"They hit me some, I reckon," he acknowledged.

"Hit you some!" Jim exclaimed. "I thought you never was goin' to fall down."

"What happened?"

"There was a couple of jaspers hidin' behind those curtains at the end of the room, and three more in a room acrost the hall—jest in case, I reckon. Lars an' me tried to help, but you didn't have a chanct to start with. Only thing is, it all happened so durn quick an' you was so fast you like to have killed Varro before the others could think to move. You ought to have heard that crazy buzzard rave, afterwards, when he got his voice back."

"You stopped pock-face for me," Silver said, remembering.

"Stopped him plenty," Jim Clane concurred briefly. "Busted his lower belly. He died. Lars tried to git at this Black Juan that was hammerin' you, but one of the others tripped him an' another of 'em wrapped a gunbarrel aroun' my neck. We couldn't do much with our hands tied."

A faint, familiar voice came from a darkened corner. "I am sorry to see you here, my son. I prayed that you would not come, but God willed it otherwise."

Silver's heart lifted suddenly. "Padre Pete!" His voice was warm with affection. "Are you all right, Padre."

"Quite all right, *amigo mio.*" Padre Pete's answer was placid.

They been torturin' him," Lars Johanssen growled.

Silver cursed savagely, and then apologized to the priest.

Padre Pete chuckled. "It is better to hear a good man curse than an evil one pray," he quoted.

"Ah, Padre," Silver smiled, "there is more rejoicing in heaven...."

"Yes, yes," the priest returned hastily. "The sinner is not evil—only his sin. But I think at last I have seen a man whom Satan has made wholly his own."

"Where is Gracia?" It had been the first question on Silver's lips, but he had not had the courage to ask it.

"They kept her here for a while—until she—er—fainted," The priest returned. "Then they took her away—I think to worry me. I don't believe they have—harmed her, yet."

"No," Silver said grimly. "I suppose that is a pleasure reserved for me to witness."

He stood up restlessly, impatience rioting through him. There was not much time to lose. He found then that his feet were bound to the wall by a length of chain.

"No use, Silver." Jim Clane appeared to have read his thought. His voice was a little tight, and regretful. "We're in a room at the top of the house. That window opens onto a sheer drop that runs a hundred feet to the ravine below. A little drop onto those rocks would fix a man plenty. Besides which, there's been a guard across the ravine, with a Winchester. I s'pose just in case we managed to make a rope out of this stone floor."

Silver's eyes sought the door—the only other exit from the room.

"Solid oak, four inches thick an' iron-bound," Jim said laconically. "Big bolt on the outside. Gratin' at the bottom to shove stuff in here, an' two men on guard outside."

A COLDNESS struck at Silver Trent, circling his stomach, sending a chill along his spine. Yet if fear sat below his breastbone, the coolness in his mind was of another stuff. Only after a while, there began to be a little desperation in the circling of that mind.

This thing looked unbeatable. No matter where he looked there was, figuratively as well as literally, a blank wall.

After a moment he called out softly, "Hola, friends at the door! It is I, El Halcon de la Sierra, who speaks."

One of the guards laughed. "You are no hawk, but a dead dog," he taunted. "Therefore do not speak."

"I am not yet dead," Silver answered, his temper leashed. "Would you like to be rich?"

"Silence, pig!" the other guard snapped. "Do you think we also want to die?"

"Help me to get out of here, and I promise to take you with me safely out of Varro's reach. Then I will give you enough silver so that you and your family to your mother's cousins may live in luxury the rest of your lives. And my word is still the word of El Halcon, which no man has known to be broken."

A cold chuckle came from the other side of the door. An instant later a key turned in the lock. The great bar outside creaked and the door swung inward. El Diablo stood there, a lantern lighting his hunched form and painting satanic shadows across his dark face. Black Juan stood behind him.

"It is a pity that these poor devils have not the keys, either to the door or to your chains," he said tauntingly. "Also, I don't think they would be happy with all that money. The certainty of death would take the taste from the food and the savor from the wind."

Silver laughed a little grimly. "I think they need not be afraid. I promise to kill you, Varro, before I leave this place—for what you have done to Padre Pete, if for no other reason."

Varro looked coldly amused. "His own fault, I'm afraid. He was just a little stubborn about telling me who the girl was."

"I didn't tell, Silver," Padre Pete put in quickly.

Varro laid a wicked glance on him. "It wasn't necessary," he said softly. "If my guess had not been right you wouldn't have stood so much torture."

Silver's throat closed up suddenly. "You devil!" he ground out.

Varro's face was suddenly envenomed.

"You'll think so in a minute," he snarled. "My men are riding tonight. Not a hundred, but twice that many. They are going for one last raid on the border, in case your cow-clowns are interested. It will be the cleanup. I promise that there won't be a gringo spread within the Ace Bend country that will not lose its treasure, its cattle, and its very existence. But before they go that far, they'll stop on the way and wipe out that snake's nest of yours, Trent. Think that over. I'm going now to see them off and give them their last orders. Then I'll bring the girl here—to amuse us!"

An evil, hating triumph flamed in his eyes. "This night will be the real beginning of Esteban Varro's power," he cried, exalted. "Greenbacks, fat cattle, and the death of the one man who might have—annoyed me. Ah, damn your puling soul to Hell, but I would give that power, and every other thing I own, for the pleasure I'm going to have this night. That's how much I value the sheer joy of wrecking that arrogant mind of yours and pulling the sniveling pious soul from your body, the way I will pull your fingernails from the screaming flesh beneath them!"

He turned and swung out. The door slammed heavily behind him and the lock and bar grated into place.

Silver stood for a moment, his eyes narrowed, his solid lips making a long grim line under the aquiline nose. There was a glister of sweat on his upper lip, invisible, he hoped, in the darkling room. He knew that for the first time in his life he was feeling fear—the paralyzing fear that claws at the sickened stomach and puts a cold heaviness into the limbs and the mind.

He fought to keep from visualizing in advance the thing he was about to witness. Garcia, dishonored, tortured, killed. Beside that his own death seemed a small thing—something to be welcomed. Ah, this Esteban Varro knew his man all right. It was as though the evil and the hatred in him flared, incandescent, into second sight.

A shudder, slow, violent, shook Silver's body, and a bitter fire began to burn through his veins. This was his night for learning things. He had already learned fear. Now, it appeared, he was learning hatred. He had thought he had known how to feel that. But all he had ever known was a kind of acute dislike. This corroding, blazing, acid-eating thing, made up of helpless fury, of poisonous loathing and concentrated murder, was something he had never conceived.

A pale orange glow had begun to fill the room. Through the window, he could see the great yellow disk of the moon coming up over the ravine.

SILVER MOVED suddenly toward the window. The length of his leg-chain barely let him reach it. It was at the height of his chest, and the bars were set wide enough so that a man's head could get between them. He thrust his head out, looking down.

Below, in the moonglow, the sheer wall of the building dropped windowless to the of the ravine. The building was flush with the granite ledge, so that the drop ran on down, straight, to the bottom. There, rushing water foamed white around jagged rocks, upthrust like dark and shadowy fangs, waiting.

It was a dizzy height, with certain death at the bottom. Watching the lines of the building and the ravine converge down into those depths put a sudden swimming in Silver's head.

For a moment, his moist palms gripped the cement ledge of the window sill, as though he were hanging on. Then, slowly, his will forced his body to relax, his brain to steady. His eyes examined the rear elevation of the house, noting windows, the moon-shadowed cracks of the rough stonework.

On the other side of him, Lars Johanssen stirred restlessly, his chains clanking a little.

"Come here, Lars," Silver whispered.

The big man stepped forward. The length of his chain just letting him meet Silver.

"We've got to break my handcuffs," Silver murmured. "You'll have to help."

91

"Not a thing in the place to do it wit'," Lars muttered. "We ban lookin'."

"Take hold of my wrists and pull them apart when I give the word," Silver whispered. "Between us I think we can break them."

Lars' big chest sucked in breath a little sharply. "Cripes, hombre," he breathed. "We br'ack bones in your wrists like dot."

"No," Silver murmured. "No. I think not. Anyway, we must try. Take them. All your strength now, when I give the word."

Lars hesitated. "Mebbe we try br'ack mine," he suggested.

Silver stirred impatiently. "Do as I say," his whisper was hard.

Lars' great hands reached out and caught his wrists over the cuffs. "Tor an' Wotan!" he swore softly.

Silver stretched the chain, flexed the corded muscles of his wrists, building them into steel bars.

"Now!" he breathed.

Lars' huge arms leaped into straining rigidity, forcing the wrists apart. The great rope-like sinews of Silver's arms set, straining his arms outward. The cuffs bit into the flesh of his wrists, bit at the muscles underneath, and held, in an agony of pressure.

"More! Harder!" Silver panted through set lips.

Sweat ran streaming down his face. Every muscle in his great, cat's body stood out at full strain. Through the darkness, Lars' laboring breath was hot on his face. Yet the chain held!

"Ease and when I say so, jerk," Silver panted.

Lars eased. Took his hands away and wiped the sweat from his forehead. "By Tor, Silver," he panted. "You break yourself sure 'nough like that. Your wrists ban bleedin' already. We ban too strong, hombre. De flesh an' bone vill not stand it."

"You say you're strong," Silver taunted him contemptuously. "But you can't break a little chain, even with my help. Do as I say, and try to get something into it this time. You're more like an' old woman than a man."

Lars swore, wiped his palms on his jeans. "Come on dan," he growled harshly.

"Ready," Silver whispered, "jerk!"

The chain snapped taut, held momentarily as blood spurted from Silver's wrists, then—snapped!

CHAPTER 12
ESCAPE—TO DEATH!

SILVER STOOD an instant, breathing hard through his nose, his lips tight-closed against the involuntary groan that had come up in him. Then he stooped and caught at his leg chain. It was locked around his ankles with a padlock. His big fingers felt the lock in the dark, righted it, then tapped it sharply on the floor.

It held, but he was not worried about that. There wasn't a padlock in the world that couldn't be sprung with a tap if you knew how. He struck again, more sharply this time.

"What you do there?" a guard's voice came through the door, alarmed.

"Come in and see, if you want to know," Silver jibed.

"I don't have to see. You try something and I will shoot through this grating."

Silver tapped again, and the lock sprung open.

The grating slid back, leaving an aperture about six inches high and two feet long at the bottom of the door.

Silver laughed. "Shoot," he invited, taking a seat as though nothing had happened. "That would be better than what your master has in store for us. But I think that you will be put on the rack for spoiling his fun."

The guard cursed, and closed the grating.

Silver was on his feet like a cat. "Now, the bars," he whispered to Lars. "Two will do it. Be fast."

Lars moved fast. "Nobody can get out there," he muttered. "But, by Wotan, if you say you can, you vill!"

His great frame heaved at the center bar, Silver working with him, his back a straining arc of power, the muscles of his neck standing out like steel pillars.

No two ordinary men could have so much as bent one of those bars a little. But the strength of these two was not ordinary. The bar bent, the concrete crumbled, the iron came free.

Instantly, furiously, they attacked the next. It pulled out with a groaning creak that sent the grating at the bottom of the door back instantly.

Silver did not hesitate. He slid his boots and socks off and rose, catlike to the window.

"*Dios!* What you do?" The guard's squawk was startled, unbelieving.

Silver's legs went through the window.

The guard's sixgun blasted, thunderous in that confined space. A slug smacked the wall next to Silver's shoulder. His legs were outside now, hanging, his body going through. A hit would send him hurtling to his death, even if the bullet did not kill.

For an instant, his great shoulders caught against the side of the window and the remaining bar. The guard's gun blasted again, the bullet going low.

Silver's shoulders hunched, twisted, came free. He was hanging by his hands to the sill. The sixgun bellowed again, sending lead screaming over his head.

His toes groped for a hold on the rough stone, found it. He loosed one hand and clawed with it sideways, until the steel fingers caught in a crevice. Then he worked the foot on that side in the same direction.

A second later, he was to one side of the window, out of danger of the guard's Colt, but with nothing to cling to except the quarter-inch and half-inch crevices between the laid stones. And beneath him, vacancy.

He knew that he had a short time of grace—for the guard did not have the key to the door. One of them would have to run for help. Had run, in fact—for Silver had heard their exclamations and suddenly pounding feet.

He moved again, infinitely careful, yet swift. One mistake, one misstep now, would send him to his death. Yet he had to hurry.

Looking out, he had noted a window some distance along the wall of the house, on the same level. He could not see it now, with his face cheeked up against the stone, but it was no more

Silver felt the warmth of
blood on his flesh.

than twenty feet away. If it was not barred, and if they did not think of it in time to cut him off, and if he made no mistake....

A sharp exclamation below him, on the other side of the ravine, struck his ear. His lips tightened. The guards below had not been taken away. Their attention had undoubtedly been attracted by the shooting, but against the darkness of the window and in the deceptive light of the moon they had not made out Silver's clinging, flattened figure until now.

Silver turned his head a little to find the men. In doing so, his glance plummeted into the depths of the ravine, a dark and yawning chasm now. His spine chilled, and his head began to turn. With a jerk of his will, he pulled his fascinated eyes away from the emptiness below. One hand had loosened a little, and gingerly, hundredth of an inch by hundredth of an inch, he wormed it to a firm grip again.

From across the ravine, a Winchester shot laid its flat, keening crack on the dark air. The bullet hit two yards above Silver's head, sending a spray of rock-dust down on him.

He moved again. His hands were moist now, and his gripping toes slippery with sweat. The men across were overshooting. That was to be expected, he told himself grimly. In the dark it was natural to take too much front sight. The question was, when would the marksmen realize that, and correct.

ANOTHER SHOT whipped out, higher this time, and to the right. Silver took a long breath, steadying his nerves. Self-scorn gripped him suddenly, angering him. This was no time to get jittery and jumpy like an old woman.

He reached out hand, then foot, swiftly yet carefully, and

moved again. Another shot came, lower this time, but still to the right. He moved again, and again, knowing that he was moving into the line of fire.

A fourth shot sounded, the bullet striking at Silver's feet. He cursed softly, his back cold with the realization of what a hit there would mean. Despite himself his nerves were shaking, and his feet and hands were wet.

Desperately he clung and moved, knowing that his risk was tripled now. Clinging there to nothing, he needed all the purchase of his grip, all the friction that dry skin could give him.

The flat snarl of the Winchester ripped out again. Lead smashed at the rock an inch over Silver's right shoulder, ricocheting with a vicious scream past his cheek. He felt the hot nip of it, clung closer an instant, and then went on, feeling the warmth of blood on his flesh where the lead had scraped his skin.

Silence below. The guards, he knew, were reloading. From far-off, beyond the end of the house, faint shouts sounded. The alarm had reached the men's quarters. Had it only been that long since he started? It seemed to him that he had been flattened along that wall, clinging desperately with fingers and toes, for an eternity.

His hand reached out, groped, found no hold. For an instant, he stood tense, paralyzed. He was trapped. He would never make it back to that other window. He....

He reached upward, found a hold directly above, moved up a foot. His fingers slipped, his breath stopped. For one endless second he swayed outward, hanging over space. Death yawned for him. He had an instant's vision of his body over-ending downward, the rush of air unbreathing in his cold lungs. Then his frantic fingers caught, held.

He drew a long, shaken breath and moved sideways again. His outstretched right hand struck something smooth—the frame of the window!

Relief sent a dangerous weakness into his knees. Trembling now, because victory was in sight, he pulled himself over, got his right hand hooked around inside the window. From below, the rifle blasted and lead slugged the stone above his head. He swung to the window sill, pulled himself in. A bullet snarled past his head and chunked into the inner wall. Then he was through, tumbled onto the floor. Out of range.

For one weakened moment he lay on the floor where he had fallen, then he got to his feet, breath coming a little fast, but steady now.

The yellow moonlight showed him a bedroom, apparently empty. He paced softly to the door leading onto the upper hallway. It was empty. But below, he could hear footsteps and excited voices.

Cat-footed, he raced to the stairwell, raced down a flight to the second floor. A rush of men pounded the lower hall, hit the stairs going up. Silver saw a lighted doorway ahead of him, on the second floor hallway. He ghosted toward it.

An exclamation sounded halfway up the stairs. "Who went into that room? I saw something."

Then Varro's savage voice, behind: "Get into there then, quick! You, Carlos. And you, Juan. The rest of you go up and see what's happened upstairs."

Silver's eyes flashed around the room, looking for a hiding place, a way of escape. It was a big room, lined with books, with a door in the opposite corner, but he knew at once that he could not reach it before the searchers got there.

To his left, an alcove showed, portières half concealing it. Silver glided toward it, slipped behind a curtain, flattened back against the curving wall. As he moved, a black cat got up suspiciously from the table where the lamp was, arched his back, fur up-ending.

A paunchy, thick-necked, villainous looking man burst into the room, sixgun in hand. Another was on his heels.

"Carrao!" the first swore in deep disgust. "It was the cat."

"Search! Take no chances!" Varro's voice rattled out from the doorway. "Get to that other door, Juan. Carlos, look behind the curtains in the alcove. No, wait—he's there!" He raised his voice. "Come out, Trent, or I'll riddle you with bullets through that curtain."

SILVER HELD his breath. How could the man know he was there? His feet could not show beneath the portières, which came to the floor. For that instant, he was ready to believe that Esteban Varro really was endowed with second sight. Then the shadow of a grim smile tugged at his lips. He flattened himself further, and waited, in silence. If Varro was bluffing, he'd have to show his hand.

The sharp bellow of a sixgun filled the room, a fast double report. A bullet ripped through the curtain, grazed Silver's chest, and slapped into the wall. A second slug passed in front of his legs. Instantly the gun sounded again, but this time the two shots pierced the other curtain—and Silver knew that Varro had been bluffing!

"Juan, you fool!" The *haciendero's* voice was like a whipcrack. "What are you doing? Search that other room! Carlos, take a look behind those curtains, just to be sure. *Por Dios,* I believe that that animal does not grunt or fall merely from one bullet!"

The boots of the man called Carlos strode to the curtain. As he got there, Silver moved, his left hand flashing toward the Mexican's Colt, his right fist hooking for the jaw.

Carlos had time for one startled cry, then that driving fist caught him and he dropped like a poled beef.

Silver had the gun in his hand. At the doorway of the other room, Black Juan had whirled, Colt leveling. In that instant, Varro's Colt thundered, twice. But Silver had struck and ducked, in one swift continuous movement, as he flipped the gun in his hand. Moreover, the lamplight did not extend to him, so that he was a moving target in shadow. El Diablo's shots slapped over his head so close as to sound like the double pop of a whip.

Silver laughed in his throat, knowing that now Varro's gun was empty. The captured sixgun bucked once against his palm, driving lead at Black Juan. In the same instant, the Mexican's gun exploded, but the shot went wild. Silver had beaten him to the play by the split fraction of a second.

Black Juan grunted and went down, hitting the floor like a sack of dirt.

In that instant, Varro's long arm swept out, caught the lamp on the table and sent it hurtling toward Silver. It smashed against a corner of the alcove, but before it struck, El Diablo was flashing toward the door, a hunched, infinitely speedy black shape in the shadows.

Silver flipped a shot at him, missed. Then he, too, jumped for the door, his big body moving like a charging catamount. Something hit his leg, caught with a spitting yowl between his ankles. Silver stumbled and went heavily to his knees.

The black cat, as though it were Varro's familiar, hurtled, spitting through the doorway and disappeared on the trail of its master.

Silver leaped to his feet, but when he got to the doorway, Varro was out of sight. Casting a backward glance into the room, he saw that the spilled kerosene from the lamp had ignited the alcove curtains. Blue flame, weird and deadly, licked toward the motionless countenance of the man called Carlos.

Silver hesitated. He had no time to lose, yet in a second that flame would be at the senseless Mexican's nostrils and mouth, would lick down his throat, indrawn, to sear his lungs.

He swung back into the room quickly. The man served Esteban Varro and deserved little mercy, yet....

He reached down, caught the prone body by the ankles and jerked it away from the fire. Then he leaped to beat out the flames with his hands. He had just remembered that Gracia was in that house.

Back of him, a voice spoke. "You—you took the trouble to save me?" The man, Carlos, was sitting up with a dazed expression on his face. "I—I saw the fire coming toward me. Maybe I could have moved," he muttered. "But you—you didn't know that."

"Maybe I should have let you burn," Silver told him crisply, "since you serve a devil. Thank whatever devil saints you have that I could not."

He started for the door, whirled at a sudden thought. "Where's the girl kept?" he snapped. "Talk fast, if you value that dog's hide of yours."

Upstairs, at the end of the hallway, he could hear Varro's voice, and the quick trampling of feet. He had not an instant to spare. They were coming for him. He put his Colt muzzle to the Mexican's temple. "Quick!"

"No, need, Señor," Carlos Figuero told him, tight-voiced. "God and my dear wife forgive, I would tell you anyhow. Quick, and I'll show you. By chance I learned this afternoon."

He caught Silver's arm and led him swiftly toward the inner door. As they passed him, Black Juan stirred and groaned.

They went through the inner room and out a door that led onto a corridor, which was evidently an L-extension of the one which opened onto the big library.

From the library, they could hear Varro's voice, cursing, ordering a search.

Breathless, ghostlike, they went down the hallway to some back stairs and up these stairs to the third floor again.

Silver knew at the top that they were near the room in which he had been imprisoned, but at the front of the house. Carlos stopped before a door, casting a frightened glance over his shoulder. "Here," he whispered.

Silver tried the door. It was locked.

CHAPTER 13
A DESPERATE CHOICE

S ILVER'S JAW tightened. It was an ordinary door, not like the heavy oak of the prison room. The noise of opening it would be heard, but he had no choice.

He stood back and then hurled his shoulder into it. The wood splintered. The lock yielded with a crack, and the door swung inward. The noise had not been as great as he had expected.

Inside, the room was lighted, and Gracia was there!

Her gasp of thanksgiving greeted him, "Silver!"

She was tied to the bed. He moved toward her swiftly, followed by Carlos. The Mexican already had his knife in his hand. He was shaking with excitement, and his face seemed bloodless, but his mouth was stern and his eyes were steady.

"No time to waste, Señor," he murmured in quick warning.

Silver nodded, waiting in silence while he cut the ropes that bound the girl. She stood with difficulty, but she could move.

"Can you get her out of here?" Silver asked rapidly.

"I think so, Señor. We must go back down the stairs. You are not coming?"

Silver's nails were biting into his palms. More than anything on earth he wanted to see this girl safely away. Could he trust her with this Mexican? The man looked honest enough and he had helped so far, yet Silver's gun muzzle had never been far from him, in case of treachery. But if he followed his heart, he would be leaving Lars and Jim and the Padre at the mercy of Varro. They had risked this with him. They were his men.

"No," he murmured through set teeth. And then, "Quickly now. I'll see you down the stairs."

He did not understand why nobody had heard the door and come to investigate. Yet only seconds had passed, and the searchers themselves were making so much noise that they might not have been able to locate that cracking sound instantly.

They went down the stairs swiftly and unseen, until they got to the second floor. Then voices below warned them that a party was coming up.

Silver looked around him hastily. Other voices were at the end of the corridor. A door nearby opened into a room on the front of the house. He tried it. It gave instantly. Swiftly he herded the others in. The door closed behind him just as the party at the end of the corridor came around the corner.

The room was dark and unoccupied. Silver hurried to the window and breathed easier when he saw that it was unbarred. Below, the drop to the garden was not great.

"Out with you, first," he whispered to Carlos. "I'll hand the señorita down to you. Guard her with your life, man."

"I'm not going," Gracia's voice came breathless but determined.

"Yes. Quickly, Gracia. You must."

"I won't go without you, Silver."

"I can't leave without the others. Please, dar—Gracia. Don't waste my time. You've got to go in a hurry."

"If you are going to help the others, I will go also. I'm not going to leave you."

His sudden fingers bit into the flesh of her shoulder. "Varro is sending two hundred men," he said swiftly, "to wipe out our crowd. They've already left. Even now, you'll have to short-cut and kill a horse getting to warn them. Go. Do you understand? I command it."

Upstairs, Varro's screeched curse rang out. He had discovered the loss of Gracia!

Silver swung on Carlos, his low voice suddenly savage. "Get out that window. And stick to her, or I'll have your heart. Here— here's your gun. Use it when you have to."

The Mexican moved swiftly. For a moment his form was silhouetted, then he dropped with a soft thud to the earth below.

Silver caught Gracia up into his arms. "No—no!" she murmured desperately, but he did not listen. He set her on the window sill, caught her wrists and lowered her. Leaning far out, he could make her fall only a few feet.

He watched while the pair of them disappeared into the shadows of the garden, and breathed a prayer that they would get free. Yet his lips were dry from the fear that they might not, that she might again fall into the hands of Esteban Varro. Already footsteps were pounding down the stairs.

HE WAITED until he heard the footsteps on the stairs quieting. Then he slid out and took the stairs going up. Somewhere below, he could hear Varro's raving, cursing voice.

He wished that he had a gun, but there was no time to think of getting one. This whole thing had happened so quickly that Varro had not had a chance to get things organized. He would do so now, and promptly. Silver's mind raced, trying to foresee El Diablo's actions.

When he had discovered Gracia's escape, he had, evidently, raced for the ground floor in an attempt to cut her and Silver off. He would be having the garden searched now, would throw a cordon around the house. Then, with the rest of his men, he would come to make a thorough, floor to floor search of the house, leaving men in each searched part, to see that Silver could not do now what luck had actually enabled him to do before: slip from floor to floor, avoiding the searchers.

Cat-footed, Silver moved down the corridor to the corner which led to the room where the others were imprisoned. He heard voices, and a cautious look showed him that the two guards had been left at the door. They were standing within two yards of him, one with his back to him, the other leaning against the wall.

"I think they are wasting time," one of them said. "Once in the garden, he would get away. The man's the devil himself."

"Curse him," the other snarled. "If he gets free, we'll have the skin taken off our backs with a whip."

"It was not our fault," the other muttered suddenly. "We did not have the key to the—*awk!*"

His jaw-dropped head snapped back against the wall, as the other guard's hurtled body hit him. Silver had pounced around the corner like a mountain cat striking. His outthrust hand had caught the man who had his back turned and hurled him into his partner. Now Silver's great hands slapped their heads together again, with a sound like great eggs cracking. Simultaneously, the two bodies went limp, dropped to the floor.

Swiftly, Silver reached for their guns, buckled on one belt, took the other in his hand. He had been afraid he would have to break the lock with gunfire, but in the excitement the great iron key had been left in it. He lifted the bar, turned the key and went in, leaving the door open, so it could not be unexpectedly bolted behind him.

"Silver!" Jim Clane's voice was a shaken curse of triumph.

Lars Johanssen growled deep in his throat, on a note which told that he could not find voice. Only Padre Pete sounded unexcited.

"God is very good, my son," he said gently.

Silver wasted no words, but knelt to jar Lars' padlock open. He was shaken now, with a sinking feeling deep in his stomach. He could hear voices coming up the stairs—up both stairs! To be this close, and not be able to save them....

He cursed softly with relief, for Lars Johanssen kicked instantly free of his leg chain.

"I knew that padlock trick too," Jim Clane said. "We kept the chains on, but was ready for a quick break. Only Padre Pete's lock wouldn't come loose."

Silver jumped for Padre Pete. The voices were closer now. He rapped the lock sharply on the floor. Nothing happened. Sweat sprang out on his forehead. He tried again. The voices and footsteps were at the head of the stairs now. His hand crashed down savagely. The lock smashed, sprang.

He leaped to the door. A group of half a dozen were coming along the hall. His guns bucked against his palms, filled the hallway with sudden, crashing thunder.

Two men went down, one clasping a smashed thigh, the other

sitting, ghost-faced, with his hand clawing at his shoulder. The other four were tumbling over themselves in a mad rush for the stairway.

To the left, a sixgun blasted. The slug hammered into the edge of the wooden door. The crowd from the backstairs had gotten there. Silver stepped back a little and sent a shot crashing into the one lantern which hung from the ceiling of the hallway. It smashed, and a half darkness filled the corridor. But light still came from around the corner to the left—and that was bad.

AT THE right, the panic-stricken rush had halted at the head of the stairs and Silver could hear Varro's voice cursing, trying to drive them to rush the prison room, and shouting for help to his men below.

Silver knew that the four men there would be crouched now on the stairs, ready to sweep the hallways with lead the instant anyone stepped out into it. He knew, too, that he would be outlined against the light from the left, a perfect target. It looked like checkmate. Yet they could not stay there to be trapped in the prison room.

Over his shoulder he murmured to the others: "I'm going to put out that light. Stay here until I call you."

He eased to the door. Hands, gun-filled, showed at the head of the stair well. He slammed two shots at them.

A startled Mexican went down under Silver's running bullet. Behind Silver the guns began to roar in a sharp volley.

A bullet took him in the thigh, sent him staggering forward on hands and knees. Lead howled and whined over him. Above him a Mexican loomed, sixgun leveled, and Silver, with both guns in his hands on the floor, knew that he was a dead man.

Back of the corner a gun crashed. The Mex who was about to shoot Silver jerked as though shaken by a strong wind, threw up his hands and fell backwards.

A panicky shout of curses filled the air. The hammer of guns around the corner turned into staccato thunder. Silver crouched, brought his guns up and moved forward, putting full weight on his wounded leg.

A yelling Varro man jumped into view, dropped his guns and put his hands over his head in surrender. A bullet screaming from the stairhead cut him down.

Silver whirled around the corner, saw one man with his hands up, and a tangle of others on the floor. Beyond them stood Carlos Figuero and—Gracia! Both held smoking guns in their hands.

Silver cursed softly, divided between regret and thankfulness and admiration.

He whirled again, eased his head around the corner and saw that he could make out the men firing from the stair well. He shot twice, fast. One man staggered upward, clutching his neck near his shoulder. Another, hit squarely in the head, dropped forward. The others ducked under cover.

"Come on," Silver yelled to the three in the prison room.

They came with a rush. At the stairhead a man jerked upward, leveling his gun. Silver shot past Jim Clane's shoulder, and split the Varro man's breastbone with the shot.

The three sped around the corner then, out of range. Silver

gestured to the fallen Mexicans and the one who had surrendered. "Get your guns from these."

Awkwardly, hands still manacled, they did so, while Silver hastily buckled cartridge belts around them. They went down the stairs fast, to the second floor. Feet were already pounding on the stairs coming up.

"In here," Silver snapped, and made for the open door of the room through which Carlos and Gracia had first escaped.

One by one, they hurtled through the window, dropping to the garden earth below. But as Jim Clane, who was fifth, hit the ground, a party of Varro's men rushed out the front door—a dozen of them in all, and opened fire.

Silver flung himself out, landed catlike and went into action. They were crouched in an angle of the building, the wall of a short wing behind them, the main front of the house on their right. Rose bushes and cannas gave them cover.

"Edge left," he directed, "then break across the walk and keep moving through the garden." They could not afford to stay where they were a moment longer than necessary.

But he had no sooner spoken than voices and footsteps sounded around the short wing, and guns began to talk from the direction in which he meant to head.

Trapped! They had the house behind them on two sides, and a good two dozen men circling the front!

CHAPTER 14
HELL'S HAWKS

S ILVER GROANED. This was a situation from which no strategy could deliver them. To make a dash for it in the face of that many guns would be virtual suicide. The instant they left cover they would be cut down like rats. If one or two of them got through, then those two would probably be run down before they had gone twenty yards and shot from behind.

And Gracia was in the midst of this!

Even now a murderous hail of lead was concentrating on the bushes behind which they crouched. It was only luck that no one had been hit so far.

"Get down! Get down behind me," Silver breathed hurriedly to Gracia.

The girl shook her head. Her face, in the dim light from the house, was pale, but her lips were firm and her eyes blazing. "No!" she said. "I fight with you. Do you want them to kill you while I'm left here for them to get again? I'll fight with you, and I'll save a bullet for myself in case we lose."

In case they lost! Little chance now that they wouldn't, Silver thought bitterly.

On his right, Carlos Figuero said, "She would not listen to me, Señor. I couldn't keep her from coming back."

Silver's voice gentled. "I told you to stick to her, and you did—amigo."

Carlos' head came up, with pride in the movement. "Señor,"

113

he said softly, "I think we will not ride again, but—if I could ride with you…."

"You can!" Silver's voice had a sudden ring in it. "We'll beat this, somehow."

He crept forward, peering between two bushes. Lashed by Varro's voice, the hacienda men were creeping forward. Tight-mouthed, narrow-eyed, Silver picked the two nearest, and his guns bucked in a double report.

An instant crash of gunfire answered the flashes of his Colts, but Silver had rolled.

Then from in front, from all sides, they were coming forward. A running rush, closing in. The defenders' guns were going desperately, but it was the end, and all knew it. No six could stand against odds like that!

"To Silver! *A nos otros, Los Halcones!* Hell's Hawks for Trent!"

Ringing, savage, the cry lifted. It sounded high above the sudden thunder of hoofs, it soared to ring, wild and fierce, against the very stars. The battle cry of Silver's men!

In brazen-clanging Spanish and hard-bitten American—a sound like a trumpet call, that the desert knew and quivered to, that the mountains had flung back triumphantly in a hundred slashing whirling fights, that echoed still, fearfully, in the dreams of men who had listened to it and lived to tell the tale.

"To Silver! Hell's Hawks for Trent!" And now the sudden, staccato thunder of the guns!

For one short instant, Silver Trent's chin dropped on his chest, and his shoulders sagged a little. Then his head came up, as a king's might, and in the darkness there was a moisture over his eyes. His crew had disobeyed him. They had no business being here. But he might have known they would. They must have started to town almost as soon as he, but knowing the roads were watched they had had to circle wide, take the long, precipitous trailless way through the mountains.

He cursed softly. "I'll have their hides for this!" But the light in his eyes belied him.

The indriving rush of Varro's men had checked suddenly. For a shocked, paralyzed moment, the guns were still. And in that momentary silence, Magpie Meyer's bubbling Indian yell lifted shrill and somehow blood-curdling. Beside him a bellowing bull voice sounded.

"Odd's thunder! Turn and fight, you rascally dogs! By the britches of my grandfather...." And by the side of that, Paolo's ecstatic howl, hurling magnificent blasphemies at the skies.

Padre Pete's softly laughing voice sounded. "I think our little Paul is saying his prayers, no?" he chuckled.

THEY COULD see the crew now, a dozen of them, flashing between the border of cottonwoods, racing into the garden itself. A dozen dark figures, moon-silvered, who sat hurtling, leaping broncos as though grown from them; crashing through the garden rows, soaring over bushes.

Silver was on his feet, his full-lunged shout a clarion of pride, *"Aqui, Los Halcones!* To me!"

A savage triumphant yell ripped up from the charging riders.

"Take them now!" Silver snapped to the men at his side. Then his guns were beating a hell's tattoo of death for the cursing Varro men.

They broke, scattering, every man for himself, in a frenzied effort to escape that racketing charge and the deadly nearer guns that hammered at them.

The charge drove straight to Silver. At the head of it, Magpie threw up his hand. The horses came to a skidding, rearing, head-fighting halt in a shower of gravel on the wide garden walk.

Silver ran forward. "Spread and ride them down," he yelled. "Varro is here. Get him. Magpie, take Gracia and keep her clear of this."

The riders had not waited for him to finish. They whirled, splitting into two groups, riding hell-for-leather on the heels of the running Varro men. Magpie groaned, caught himself, and pulled Gracia up behind him.

To Silver's left, a form lifted cautiously, a cold-snarling face sighting behind a heavy Colt. Silver whirled, knew that he was too late. But out of the darkness a cassocked, bandy-legged form catapulted. Manacled hands holding a sixgun flashed up and then down. The Varro man collapsed.

Silver tossed a brief grin at the white-haloed form that had saved his life. "Thanks, Padre," he said. Then, stuffing cartridges into his gun, he ran forward.

In front of him, circling about him and behind him, his men were riding a rigadoon of death, to the booming music of the guns, in and out the garden paths.

Two Varro men tossed down their guns, lifted their hands high, begging quarter.

Ricardo Juarez' gay laughter rang out. "You ride for the Devil and then ask mercy of me? But I do not trust you—*friends!*"

He leaned down from his horse and his gun-barrel chopped once and again. One after another the Varro men dropped, senseless. "Sleep well, *hijos mios,*" Ricardo said.

Silver ran on. He was beyond the fight now, his searching glance plumbing the night for El Diablo. Instinct turned his footsteps toward the corral. Halfway there, he saw a horse jump from beside the bars—jump from a standstill into a full run. Astride him, sat a black hunched figure, bent low.

Silver's teeth bit together. Varro! His hand flashed up and sent snarling lead after the fleeing figure until his gun was emptied.

The bullets must have come close, for El Diablo turned in the saddle, waving a mocking arm. "Another day, Trent!" his harsh yell came back. And then the powerful horse was no more than the ghost of a moving shadow across the range

"*Aqui, Los Halcones.* To me!" Silver's great shout rang out.

He thought he had seen El Diablo's horse spurt forward, as though he had been stung, after one of the shots. If the animal was hit, it might yet be possible to ride Varro down. And for once in his life, Silver Trent was ready to run a man down like a rabbit and mercilessly cut his life away!

The Trent men came, panting, laughing, the joy of the fight still running high in their veins. Silver's own horse, with Jim's and Lar's, were in the corral. Swift hands saddled them, while others were chiseling the men free of their handcuffs. Except for a couple of superficial bullet-slashes and scrapes the Trent crowd was unhurt. Scared men shoot badly.

Silver led them at a fast pace on the trail toward Sangre. At the pass, where there might have been guards, they did not reconnoiter, but swung into a charging gallop. But no guards were there. No doubt, they had gone with Varro, or deserted after he had passed.

Once past the badlands, Carlos Figuero rode up beside Silver. Rapidly, he told how and why he had that day gone into Varro's service. "I have to leave you now, and get my wife and son out of this country, before that devil has a chance to get at them," he said apologetically.

SILVER RODE an instant in thoughtful silence. It was apparent by this time that Varro's mount had been no more than creased, if he had been hit at all. There was small chance of overtaking him, or coming upon him in the dark.

"We'll go with you," He told Carlos briefly. "You can bring your family up to the hideout. Gracia and the Padre will have to live there now. It would be well to have another woman there." His keen gray glance searched the Mexican's face. "That is—if you like. You said something a while ago to the effect that you might like to ride with us. There's nothing to hold you to that, if you'd like to change your mind."

Carlos Figuero lifted his elated face to the moonlight and laughed aloud.

"Change my mind!" he cried. "Where is there a poor man in this country who would not give his right hand to ride with the Hawk of the Sierra?"

Silver was silent a moment, then he said softly, "You think that?"

"I could raise a dozen—and good men, too—in Sangre tonight!"

Silver Trent laughed a little grimly. "Maybe I'll ask you to," he said, and was silent.

His mind had gone to the country north of the border, to the Ace Bend country—fat cattle land, where there were one or two big spreads, but mostly little or medium sized ones, run by honest men who had put everything they possessed into the land—money and heart and hopes.

Toward them, destruction rode—more deadly ruinous than a ravening swarm of locusts. Two hundred men who were led now by the Devil in person—two hundred men with robbery, and rapine and murder in their hearts. They would sweep that range clean of cattle and of men. No woman would be safe and no honor sacred.

At Carlos' place, the Mexican picked up his wife, a grave-eyed, comely woman who could not conceal her relief at sight of her man. She came with them without question, riding with her little boy in her arms—a sturdy, handsome youngster.

From there, they turned straight into the hills, riding for the hideout—for Magpie had told Silver that the rest of his men had gone up there. After leaving Sangre, when Silver had gone with Jim and Lars toward the hacienda, they had ridden fast to the temporary camp, changed horses. They had detailed men to take the wounded to the hideout, and hit through the mountains, as Silver had guessed.

They had not ridden more than a mile from Carlos' place when Jim Clane and Lars and Dave Dennison rode alongside.

"Silver," Jim's voice was tight, "I'm sorry, but we've got to quit you. We got to get to the border to warn our people that those devils are comin'—an' there's no time to lose."

Silver felt a warmth come into him. You could pretty well count on these boys when the pinches came, he thought. They'd do all right, to ride the river with.

"There's no time to lose, but there's some to gain," he said. "The border's four days hard ride away. We need fresh mounts and a remuda of led-horses if we're to make time. And we have to, because Varro's got a change of horses staked out along the trail. And we need the rest of the crowd—all the men we can get—if we're to do any good when we get there."

Jim Clane swallowed. "You—you mean you're taking the crowd—to tackle an army like Varro's?"

The beginning of a smile twisted Silver's lips. "We'll whittle 'em down to our size," he answered gently.

CHAPTER 15
TO THE KILL!

THE HERD began to mill uneasily, a black formless splotch against the star-dark Texas ground. A nearby steer snorted, flinging up his head.

"Now what in hell you reckon is the matter with them cows?" Pete Neher asked, wonderingly.

"Durn if I know," Mike Blanton grumbled. "A cow-critter is too dumb fer a man to explain anythin' about. I've seed 'em stand steady in the face of hell an' destruction, an' then spook up because they smelled a ghost in the air."

"Whatever it is, we better sing 'em some," Neher replied. "If we let this herd stampede, Mort Jenkins will skin us alive.

His voice lifted unmelodiously in song.

Behind him, a black shadow materialized out of the night. Another followed, and another. Muffled hoofs moved slowly and soundlessly on the grass-cushioned earth.

Mike Blanton's horse snorted, swinging its head. Mike glanced over his shoulder uneasily.

"Hey!" he exclaimed, startled. And then, "Ugh!" as a thrown knife sank between his shoulder blades.

Pete Neher's song broke off. "What's bitin' you?" he began. "God!"

His hand clawed for his gun, but a sudden storm of Colt-fire riddled him....

Up at the ranchhouse, two miles away, Mort Jenkins looked up, his eyes narrowing, his grizzled mustache bristling a little. A faint rattle of gunfire had sounded.

"Now what?" he growled.

Myra Jenkins' cheeks paled a little. "Did that come from the direction of the herd, Mort?"

Mort Jenkins got up and turned out the light. "Stay inside," he said gruffly.

He buckled on his gunbelt and walked out, stood listening in front of the door.

Will Labat, his foreman walked around the side of the house. "You hear it, too?"

Out in front, something stirred.

"Who's out there?" Mort called sharply.

There was no answer, but now the scuff of horses' hoofs in the grass made a minor sound in the night. The dark movement became a shadowy line of riders.

"Speak up, or I'll let you have it," Mort called tensely.

Flame blossomed against the night, followed by a rattling hail of fire. Lead plucked at Mort Jenkins' shirt, slammed into the wall back of him.

Cursing, he snapped the door open and hurled himself in.

Will Labat came running around the corner of the house, his gun blasting. A slug took him, whirled him. Another smacked him face downward into the dust.

Out in back the cowhands were cursing, as gunfire ripped at them. The house was surrounded.

"Inside! Inside the house!" Mort Jenkins yelled.

The back door burst open and men came tumbling in. Five of them. A sixth lay silent in the space between the house and the bunkshack.

Lead stormed around the house. Outside, the night was an insanity of cackling gunfire. Bullets keened through the windows, smacked into the inner walls.

"Great God from Buckley," a puncher swore, "the' must be five hundred of 'em!"

"Then we'll kill four hundred and ninety an' hang the rest," Mort Jenkins said between his teeth. "Everybody take a window."

His sixgun began to go, driving lead at the shadowy forms backing the gun-flashes. A whooping group of riders drove for the window, guns blaring.

Mort Jenkins narrowed his eyes and shot four times, spaced.

When he had done, three saddles were empty, and the charge veered off, thundered back into the night.

"Bet that's the last time they try that," the rancher said with grim satisfaction. But even as he spoke, the snarl of lead around his ears was whining to a crescendo of fury, and he knew that no amount of courage or good will could stand against an attack like this.

"They're greasers, boys," he yelled. "Not enough guts in the pack to fit out a grade B louse. Give 'em hell."

So his voice yelled encouragement, but he did not look at his wife, at his side now, handing him a loaded gun. He could not bear to.

THE ATTACKERS had drawn off now. It was difficult to get a decent shot at them. But their fire had not slackened. Even putting an eye to the window corner was to invite instant death, so concentrated was the pattern of lead that hornetted through.

Then suddenly, at a shouted order, the firing slackened, ceased altogether. Mort Jenkins swore wonderingly. What was the idea now?

An exclamation from a rear window sent him toward it. He cursed. The bunkhouse was on fire!

He realized instantly that the wind was from that direction and that it would be only a matter of time before the house caught. When that happened, they would be driven out to be slaughtered.

From the darkness outside, a voice lifted, with a faint undertone of mockery in it. "Come out with your hands up, if you want to live. We'll give you this one chance."

Mort Jenkins hesitated, a sweat suddenly on his forehead. He cast an agonized glance into the room-darkness, to where his wife, Myra, stood.

But before he spoke he had made up his mind. There had been evil in the smooth run of that voice—a vibration as deadly as the *whirr* of a diamondback's rattles.

"Any of you boys that want to take a chance, can do so," Mort said, his voice harsh and a little hoarse. "Nobody can ever blame you. Anybody that stays here, is a dead man."

Inside the room a sudden silence settled, tense, almost tangible. Outside, the crackle of the flames rose, and a light grew, laying its yellow flickering through the windows and onto the floor and wall of the house.

"What you aimin' to do yourself, Mort?" a puncher asked from the stillness.

Mort Jenkins' voice came, a little shaken, a little husky. "Why, we aim to fight it out here—Myra an' me. Them cattle out there was all we had left. We—we'll stay."

He could not tell them what he had heard in that voice—the certainty of treachery and cruel evil he had felt there. These were murderers, whose word was not worth a plugged nickel. Myra must not fall into their hands....

Near him, in the darkness, he could hear the soft, quick run of his wife's breathing. Then her hand found his arm, the pressure of it gentle and comradely, in the way their years had known. He stopped his breath hard, to steady the sudden shaking of his chest, as the memory came to him of this woman's long understanding and unwavering loyalty.

In the growing fire-flicker, somebody cursed softly. Then, "I'm not droppin' out either," a voice said. "I'll play these pat."

A short breath went out around the room, as though a tension had been relaxed.

"Me, too, Slats. What do you say, boys—let's give 'em some hot lead for an answer."

"Hell, yes. Why not? Them greasers ain't goin' to leave us live anyway."

Outside, the challenge lifted again, harsher now, "Well…? You taking it, or leaving it?"

At the window, Slats Burchard said, "Leavin' it, you greasy sidewinder!" and let his gun blast, probing for the voice.

A storm of fire answered him. A bullet caught his arm and spun him back against the wall. The other's guns were going now, the acrid reek of burned powder growing thick in the house.

The bunkhouse roof burst into sudden, wind-whipped flame. From behind it, a thrown brand arced through the air, hit the edge of the roof and dropped to the ground close to the wall.

Mort Jenkins cursed through set lips. Even where it was it would probably ignite the wall. But there was nothing to do. He stuffed fresh cartridges into the hot cylinders of his guns and sent desperate lead out against the gun-flashes. Another blazing brand sailed out, but fell short. It was only a matter of time….

His thoughts broke off, shocked into immobility. For a new sound had lifted above the roar of the guns—a high-pitched bubbling yell, savage—blood-curdling.

And on top of that, a great voice, vibrant, like a clarion of fierce pride, *"A nos otros, Los Halcones!* Hell's Hawks to the kill!"

Then it struck—a storm, a whirling tornado of hammering hoofs, of full-throated savage yells, of deadly, withering gunfire.

Staring, open-mouthed, Mort Jenkins saw the ring of his enemies roll up, crack, shattering into a confusion of out-flying pieces. The fiercely burning bunkhouse lit the scene suddenly in a sharp, brilliant upflare, as though it had timed it accurately to this moment.

Mort had a glimpse of a great-shouldered figure, astride a white stallion, supple in the saddle as a riding mountain cat, and with guns deadly as lightning bolts. The firelight painted a lean, hawklike, unforgettable face, and then the great white horse was past, as the startled enemy circle broke and rolled back.

BEHIND THE big-shouldered man hurtled others—one with a curling white mustache and a wizened, wrinkled-leather face. Another long-countenanced, with high, fanatic forehead, cursing jubilantly in Spanish. Others—lean and wolflike riders, looking as though they had grown from their saddles, and with the sheer, blazing joy of battle on their dark, fierce faces.

And in that crowd there was a momentary glimpse of a blocky, tough, pugnacious figure and a huge, red-faced man whom Mort Jenkins knew well.

The rancher cursed brokenly. He ran toward the front door, flung it wide, wanting to add his guns to the attacker's strength. But the fight had already rolled out into the vast darkness beyond the firelight.

The blasting, unutterable confusion of it, the cursing of raging and frightened men, the hammering chorus of the sixguns endured a long moment. Then the fight became a rout. Panic-stricken men fled, racing in all directions, pursued by those lean, dark-faced men, as a squawking flock of chickens might be carried by a flight of hawks.

The whirling tornado of gun-flashes moved off, grew fainter, like a vortex of hell swirling into the farther darkness. And high above the fight, that big voice lifted its rallying call:

"Keep together! To me! Hell's Hawks to Trent!"

Then, as Mort Jenkins watched, a hunched, dark-cloaked figure, with a face that was a snarling mask of hatred and venom, flashed out of the darkness, alone and flattened against his horse's neck.

Instinctively, Mort's gun flashed up, as though something deep in him knew that this was not one of the rescuers but was, instead, the owner of that evil-freighted voice that had called to him out of the night.

He shot once, and then again. But that flying figure of Hell was gone into the darkness almost before he pulled trigger, and he did not need the steady, diminishing beat of the hoofs to tell him that he had missed.

A shout from the back attracted him, and then he remembered his burning house. He ran for buckets and the well. The roof of the main building had caught now in several places, and the rear wall was alight.

Sweating, concentrated minutes later, he stopped, aware that for a brief period he had forgotten the fight and the rescue. But the fire on the roof was out now, and the bunkhouse was burning low enough so that there was not any danger from it that a little vigilance could not handle.

Beside him, her comely, kindly face flushed, was Myra, an empty bucket in her hand and her cheek smudged black. He took her into his arms.

Hoofbeats came out of the darkness, at a leisurely canter now, and he looked up to see Jim Clane ride out into the shrunken glow of the firelight.

Mort Jenkins took a long breath. "Boy," he said, "Boy, I'm glad to see you!"

Behind Jim, Lars Johanssen appeared. He grinned. "We ban tank you won't be so glad," he said.

"Yeah," Jim said, "We heard we was kind of outside the law in these parts. That everybody thought we killed the two men left with the herd and made off with it."

Mort Jenkins shook his head. "We never believed it, boys," he said. "The sheriff was suspicious, but we didn't figger you had it in you to pull anythin' like that. And now—well, I saw you in that bunch that rode in. Tell me, what's happened to you. Light down. Your jobs, an' better ones, are right here waitin' for you."

For a moment, Jim Clane's face bore a trace of regret, then his smile drove it away. "I'm sorry, Mort, but Lars an' me have got another job now," he said, "an' our talk'll have to wait. Silver's waitin' down there, an' we've got to get back."

"Silver—Silver Trent," Mort Jenkins muttered. "So that's who that fightin' devil is. I've heard about him, plenty."

"Jim, Lars!" Myra Jenkins' soft voice was motherly, protesting. "You don't have to stay in that now. Silver Trent's an outlaw. You boys have got to stay inside the law."

Jim Clane looked at her. "He's an outlaw, all right, Mother

Jenkins, but he's more than that—he's everythin' a man would like to tie to. We're sorry to leave you, but…."

"Yeah, ve have new job now," Lars said softly.

Jim's mouth opened, then closed again. There were things buzzing in his head to say—explanations—words about a higher law, one that might not be necessary always but that was needed now, words that might give some idea of what it meant to be among those whose privilege it was to ride with Silver Trent— words…. And then he knew that even a week ago, he, himself would not have understood.

Out of the darkness back of him ripped a faint, high-pitched, summoning call. He threw up his hand suddenly in the Indian gesture of greeting and farewell.

"*Hasta la vista, amigos,*" he said, and whirled his horse.

"Hey! You might tell this Silver Trent that I'll be rememberin' him, Son," Mort Jenkins yelled.

Afterwards, the rancher and his wife stood for a long moment, listening to the receding hoofbeats in silence. Then Mort Jenkins turned, looking down into his wife's faintly worried eyes.

"I don't jest figger it, myself, Honey," he said, "But I wouldn't worry any. What those boys do is apt to be pretty near right, an'—well, this Trent is a man—if ever I laid my eyes on one!"

POPULAR HERO PULPS AVAILABLE NOW:

THE SPIDER
- ❏ #1: The Spider Strikes — $13.95
- ❏ #2: The Wheel of Death — $13.95
- ❏ #3: Wings of the Black Death — $13.95
- ❏ #4: City of Flaming Shadows — $13.95
- ❏ #5: Empire of Doom! — $13.95
- ❏ #6: Citadel of Hell — $13.95
- ❏ #7: The Serpent of Destruction — $13.95
- ❏ #8: The Mad Horde — $13.95
- ❏ #9: Satan's Death Blast — $13.95
- ❏ #10: The Corpse Cargo — $13.95
- ❏ #11: Prince of the Red Looters — $13.95
- ❏ #12: Reign of the Silver Terror — $13.95
- ❏ #13: Builders of the Dark Empire — $13.95
- ❏ #14: Death's Crimson Juggernaut — $13.95
- ❏ #15: The Red Death Rain — $13.95
- ❏ #16: The City Destroyer — $13.95
- ❏ #17: The Pain Master — $13.95
- ❏ #18: The Flame Master — $13.95
- ❏ #19: Slaves of the Crime Master — $13.95
- ❏ #20: Reign of the Death Fiddler — $13.95
- ❏ #21: Hordes of the Red Butcher — $13.95
- ❏ #22: Dragon Lord of the Underworld — $13.95
- ❏ #23: Master of the Death-Madness — $13.95
- ❏ #24: King of the Red Killers — $13.95
- ❏ #25: Overlord of the Damned — $13.95
- ❏ #26: Death Reign of the Vampire King — $13.95
- ❏ #27: Emperor of the Yellow Death — $13.95
- ❏ #28: The Mayor of Hell — $13.95
- ❏ #29: Slaves of the Murder Syndicate — $13.95
- ❏ #30: Green Globes of Death — $13.95

- ❏ #31: The Cholera King — $13.95
- ❏ #32: Slaves of the Dragon — $13.95
- ❏ #33: Legions of Madness — $12.95
- ❏ #34: Laboratory of the Damned — $12.95
- ❏ #35: Satan's Sightless Legion — $12.95
- ❏ **NEW:** #36: The Coming of the Terror — $12.95

THE WESTERN RAIDER
- ❏ **NEW:** #1: Guns of the Damned — $13.95

G-8 AND HIS BATTLE ACES
- ❏ #1: The Bat Staffel — $13.95

CAPTAIN SATAN
- ❏ #1: The Mask of the Damned — $13.95
- ❏ #2: Parole for the Dead — $13.95
- ❏ #3: The Dead Man Express — $13.95
- ❏ #4: A Ghost Rides the Dawn — $13.95
- ❏ #5: The Ambassador From Hell — $13.95

DR. YEN SIN
- ❏ #1: Mystery of the Dragon's Shadow — $12.95
- ❏ #2: Mystery of the Golden Skull — $12.95
- ❏ #3: Mystery of the Singing Mummies — $12.95

POPULAR HERO PULPS AVAILABLE NOW:

THE SECRET 6
- ❏ #1: The Red Shadow $13.95
- ❏ #2: House of Walking Corpses $13.95
- ❏ #3: The Monster Murders $13.95
- ❏ #4: The Golden Alligator $13.95

CAPTAIN ZERO
- ❏ #1: City of Deadly Sleep $13.95
- ❏ #2: The Mark of Zero! $13.95
- ❏ #3: The Golden Murder Syndicate $13.95

OPERATOR 5
- ❏ #1: The Masked Invasion $13.95
- ❏ #2: The Invisible Empire $13.95
- ❏ #3: The Yellow Scourge $13.95
- ❏ #4: The Melting Death $13.95
- ❏ #5: Cavern of the Damned $13.95
- ❏ #6: Master of Broken Men $13.95
- ❏ #7: Invasion of the Dark Legions $13.95
- ❏ #8: The Green Death Mists $13.95
- ❏ #9: Legions of Starvation $13.95
- ❏ #10: The Red Invader $13.95
- ❏ #11: The League of War-Monsters $13.95
- ❏ #12: The Army of the Dead $13.95
- ❏ #13: March of the Flame Marauders $13.95
- ❏ #14: Blood Reign of the Dictator $13.95
- ❏ #15: Invasion of the Yellow Warlords $13.95
- ❏ #16: Legions of the Death Master $13.95
- ❏ #17: Hosts of the Flaming Death $13.95
- ❏ #18: Invasion of the Crimson Death Cult $13.95
- ❏ #19: Attack of the Blizzard Men $13.95

DUSTY AYRES AND HIS BATTLE BIRDS
- ❏ #1: Black Lightning! $13.95
- ❏ #2: Crimson Doom $13.95
- ❏ #3: The Purple Tornado $13.95
- ❏ #4: The Screaming Eye $13.95
- ❏ #5: The Green Thunderbolt $13.95
- ❏ #6: The Red Destroyer $13.95
- ❏ #7: The White Death $13.95
- ❏ #8: The Black Avenger $13.95
- ❏ #9: The Silver Typhoon $13.95
- ❏ #10: The Troposphere F-S $13.95
- ❏ #11: The Blue Cyclone $13.95
- ❏ #12: The Tesla Raiders $13.95

MAVERICKS
- ❏ #1: Five Against the Law $12.95
- ❏ #2: Mesquite Manhunters $12.95
- ❏ #3: Bait for the Lobo Pack $12.95
- ❏ #4: Doc Grimson's Outlaw Posse $12.95
- ❏ #5: Charlie Parr's Gunsmoke Cure $12.95

THE MYSTERIOUS WU FANG
- ❏ #1: The Case of the Six Coffins $12.95
- ❏ #2: The Case of the Scarlet Feather $12.95
- ❏ #3: The Case of the Yellow Mask $12.95
- ❏ #4: The Case of the Suicide Tomb $12.95
- ❏ #5: The Case of the Green Death $12.95
- ❏ #6: The Case of the Black Lotus $12.95
- ❏ #7: The Case of the Hidden Scourge $12.95